What's her Secret?

DESIGNATED ALPHA

CRISSY SMITH

Designated Alpha
ISBN # 978-1-78430-676-2
©Copyright Crissy Smith 2015
Cover Art by Posh Gosh ©Copyright June 2015
Interior text design by Claire Siemaszkiewicz
Totally Bound Publishing

Anthologies
Caught in the Middle: Magical Ménage

Collections
Bite Me!: Savage Love
Summer Seductions: Summers' Girl
Cloaks and Daggers: Vampire Hunter

What's her Secret?
Last Call
Designated Alpha

DESIGNATED ALPHA

Dedication

Dedicated to everyone who accepted what life threw
at them and embraced their dreams.

Chapter One

The scent of salt water hung heavy in the air as the full moon lightened the dark crashing waves. Piper Maxwell stepped from the dense woods surrounding the area and onto the cool sand of the beach. Her paws made deep impressions as she climbed down the small sandbank.

Her heart pumped a frantic tempo while her body trembled in anticipation. She'd spent a couple of hours playing alone and letting her wolf enjoy freedom. Now she would hunt down a completely different kind of prey from the rabbit she'd chased only an hour before.

Though his time she had no intention of hunting the prey for dinner.

She caught a faint trace on the light breeze of someone close and lifted her head. She breathed deeply, her nose twitching, trying to determine the direction of the smell.

There, to the right.

Piper leaped down the rest of the incline and silently stalked toward her reward.

Even in her shifted form she kept her human intelligence. However, the more time she spent in her other form, the more she could feel the wolf's instincts strengthen. She didn't know whether it was normal for her to feel her wolf getting stronger. There was no one that she could ask the hundreds of questions she had.

The only connection she had with another shifter was the man who had turned her into what she was. After running for years, six months ago Joe had found her, and she'd had to kill him to protect herself and Jace.

If she hadn't ended Joe, he would have killed her, Jace and anyone else who had gotten in his way. Still, although she knew she'd done the right thing, she had bad nights when she remembered her teeth sinking into Joe's flesh. Sometimes the nightmares were so realistic that she almost believed he was haunting her.

She stumbled over a broken log and that jolt brought her attention back to the present. She wouldn't let the memory of Joe ruin her night. She refused to go back and relive it again. While the human part of her was still mortified about what she'd done, the wolf was proud. Piper had protected her mate.

Satisfaction that she could—and did—defend her lover, had her wolf side gloating inside.

Piper pushed away the feeling by mentally blocking the thought. It had taken a lot of time for her to realize that she was able to do that.

To get control of herself once again, Piper shook her body and raced down to the shore. Her wolf enjoyed the exercise and she could use it to tire her animal out.

She knew she was going in the right direction by small catches of a familiar scent. Several yards down from where she'd started she slowed, darting a look around.

Panting, she stopped and listened.

She had no idea what her face would have looked like right then but she was smiling. The aroma of her quarry was close and she could even pick up the faint crackle from a fire.

She followed the trail up the beach farther back away from the water. The sand beneath her paws was soft and helped her move in silence. She was coming up from the south, down-wind, knowing the element of surprise was on her side. He had his back to her as he crouched over the fire poking at it with a stick.

Piper hunkered down and waited.

There was no chance that she would ever hurt this man. Jace Anderson was her mate. The word floated around in her mind and it was her wolf side that liked that word.

As a human she loved Jace as her partner. As a wolf she ached to claim him, for everyone else in the world to know that he belonged to her.

For several months she'd struggled to keep the animal instinct from doing just that. To claim Jace, she would have to bite him, and that scared her. She had no idea what consequences would come from her sinking her teeth into his flesh.

She would not let Jace be changed the way she'd been.

He straightened and tossed the stick in his hand away. Piper admired his strong, broad back. She loved to run her hands and tongue over his bulging muscles. Squirming, she bit down on her tongue to hold in the sound of her need that wanted to escape.

Piper was impatient for the man to turn toward her so that she could see his face. Considering her options, she came up with an idea. She thumped her tail against the log to her side in three quick beats before she froze again.

He turned, his gaze roaming around the fallen logs and darkness. She didn't have long before he would spot her. The muscles in her legs bunched as she prepared herself. Just as he rotated to face her fully, she pounced.

In a well-practiced move, she leaped at his chest, knocking him back. His arms closed around her as the fell to the ground. She let out a rumble as he buried his hands in her fur and held her tight. She loomed over him, running her long, rough tongue over his cheek.

"Okay," he said with a laugh and pushed her head to the side. "You got me."

Pleased, she climbed off him so he could sit up. Settling next to him, she rested her chin on his leg.

"How was your run, baby?"

Jace liked to talk to her, even if she couldn't respond back. She pawed his hand, wanting to feel it back on her.

"All right, I get it," he said petting her side again.

Piper wiggled around until she was comfortably laid out listening to Jace's voice.

"I got an email from Mitch today. He downloaded several files that he wanted me to take a look at."

Mitch Ryan was Jace's best friend whom he'd known since their Special Forces days. So far Piper hadn't met the man, but she had the feeling that soon she would no longer be able to put off the introduction. Not that she didn't want to meet him…exactly. She just knew she wasn't what anyone would expect or want for their best friend. Fully aware of her shortcomings that didn't even include the fact she turned into a freaking wolf, she was lucky to have Jace.

Jace loved her. Sometimes Piper still waited for him to catch on that she wasn't good enough to him. She was certain when his best friend was there that Mitch would point it out to Jace as well.

Time was running out and she knew it. Jace had contacted Mitch, the best hacker he knew, in hope of Mitch being able to help in their investigation on her shifter origin. There weren't many avenues they could search without drawing attention to themselves. Jace believed one hundred percent that Mitch would never betray them. Jace had saved Mitch's life not once, but twice.

Her secret would have to be revealed to a stranger for the first time, if Mitch hadn't already figured it out by what Jace had requested from him. She sure hoped that Jace knew what he was doing. As much as she wanted to find out about what she was, she still feared what would happen if the wrong person found her.

In the years she'd been on the run, she had met very few people like herself. The ones she had met had either wanted nothing to do with her or hadn't given her the chance to talk to them before disappearing. It was upsetting that she'd had the chance at getting real information from someone who knew what she was going through and had ended up disappointed every time.

Jace strongly believed that the more they could find out about her *gift*, the better chance they had at protecting themselves. Piper hadn't been so sure but over the last couple of months, Jace had talked her into looking more into it. She knew he was doing it because he loved her.

She went along with his plan for the same reason.

"I haven't had the chance to look at them yet but I thought we could do it tonight before bed," Jace continued talking, unaware of the reflection she was doing in her mind.

Each week when she transformed, she and Jace stuck to this unique ritual. She would head out right after dark and spend hours letting her wolf roam free. After that she would track down Jace and spend a good amount of time with him in her shifter form. Having her as a wolf with him was helping them both. Piper no longer feared that she would somehow hurt her mate, and Jace knew that no matter which Piper he was with, he was safe.

"Mitch also wants to come down. He can be here first thing in the morning."

She jerked her attention back to Jace. She hadn't met any of Jace's close friends yet. The few co-workers that she and Jace interacted with daily were the only people that Piper was comfortable around.

She growled, showing her displeasure. Sometimes being right sucked. They were going to have to meet.

"I know." He patted her side. "He's my best friend. I've told you how much I trust him. If he sent those files and feels the need to come down, I'm sure there is a good reason."

She pushed away from Jace and stood before stretching her legs out in front of her. She wanted to shift so she was able to talk to Jace.

Presumably understanding what she wanted, Jace gained his feet and stepped back. "Go ahead."

Piper hated this part.

In movies and fiction books the transformation back and forth between human and animal was shown to be effortless. That was very untrue for her.

It hurt to shift.

It also took several long minutes to complete the change.

She crouched low and closed her eyes tightly. Her shifting started with a tingle at the base of her spine. As her skin started to stretch, she cried out in pain. The sounds of her bones popping and reshaping were loud in the quiet night. After that, Piper never really knew what took place. It seemed like she zoned out from the hurt until she was on her hands and knees, gasping for breath.

"Shh." Jace gathered her into his arms. "It's over, baby. Calm down."

Piper clung to him as she trembled in exhaustion. God, she hated what she had to go through anytime she wanted to shift into her wolf.

Jace whispered softly to her, which helped Piper get control of herself. She pushed her bangs off her sweaty face and peered up at him.

"Hi." He smiled.

He was so handsome. Sometimes Piper would just stare at him, amazed that this wonderful man wanted her. "Hi."

He chuckled and stood, helping her to her feet. "How do you feel now?"

"I'm fine," she assured him. Her legs were still a little shaky, but she had more important things on her mind. "Did you really invite your...your friend here?"

Jace sighed before cupping her cheek. "He's not going to hurt you."

"But he knows...what I am?"

"I think he might suspect," Jace admitted. "He knows what I'm looking for but I never told him it was because of you. He does know that I didn't start looking into werewolves until after we moved in together."

"How could he even believe? It's not like this is normal conversation. What if he wants to see me? Or he could be bringing someone to take me away."

"No," Jace said before lightly kissing her. When he drew back, his gaze was soft. "I'd never let anyone hurt you. We saw some strange...things when we were overseas. Stuff that we couldn't explain. That was the reason I contacted Mitch. I knew he was already looking into some of our weird experiences."

Piper relaxed into his hold. She didn't like the thought that someone she didn't know might have guessed what she was. Even if Jace trusted this guy, it didn't mean that she would. While Jace spent time with his friend, she would have to do some of her own digging around. If this friend of Jace's tried to hurt either one of them, he would find out just how protective she could be.

"Fine," she said letting the subject drop.

"Good," he replied before he ran his hands down her side. Jace lowered his mouth to her shoulder and peppered kisses over her flesh. "Because I can think of so many other things to talk about when you're naked and at my mercy."

She grinned. "Oh yeah?"

Jace lifted her easily off her feet and strolled back closer to the fire. Wrapping her legs around his waist, she nipped at his jaw. She hadn't seen the blanket and was surprised when he laid her down on top of it. He always thought of everything.

As Jace settled between her legs Piper ran her hands over his chest. The tattoo over his heart was dark and a complicated series of intertwined lines. She loved to run her tongue over the ink and did so as Jace's fingers trailed down her neck.

She knew his body now. What he liked, how to arouse, and what was too much.

Jace tugged on her hair, lifting her face. She moved her mouth against his as they shared a deep, passionate kiss. She shivered as he ran his fingers lower down her body before tracing his fingertips against her wet folds.

Piper spread her legs farther apart before lifting her hips slightly.

Jace's erection pressed against her thigh. Naked, she wanted him naked.

Distracting her, Jace slipped one long finger inside. All thought of getting his pants off left as he plunged his digit in and out. Her nails scored his back as she bucked up, trying to get more sensation. "Please."

His breath coasted against her ear. "What?" he teased. "Tell me."

Oh, she loved it when he went dominant on her. Of course, Jace knew that. "More. I need more."

"Beg," he demanded.

Piper had no problem complying with that. She pleaded for him to take her as she snapped her hips.

"I love the sound of you begging."

She was so relieved when he pulled his hand away and started to unsnap his jeans that she almost sobbed. The ache between her legs was like a fire coursing through her body.

Unable to keep her hands to herself, she petted his broad chest. He shuddered as her fingertips brushed his nipples.

Jace finished pushing down his pants before he caught both her wrists and moved them over her head. As she bit her lip, excitement throbbed down her spine.

"Stay where I put you."

She nodded.

He released his hold before traveling down her body, kissing and nipping at her sensitive flesh. Gasping, she bucked at the sting.

"Stay."

Her breath caught at his tone. Holy hell, she was so turned on. "Jace!"

She felt his smile against her stomach but that was the only response she got. He was going to make her wait until she was desperate for him.

Digging the heels of her feet into the blanket, Piper tried her best to follow Jace's order. The submissive part of her wanted to please her lover. Pushing her own needs down was a struggle.

"Oh God."

She jumped and whimpered when his lips brushed over her clit. "Please, Jace. Please."

He spread her thighs farther apart while he licked her once. Just a taste.

Piper did sob then.

"All right, honey, it's okay," Jace said before he sat up and positioned himself at her entrance.

Moonlight glinted off the small bead of moisture at the tip of his cock. He was just as aroused as she was. Not done torturing her quite yet, he pumped himself several times while she watched.

She'd been able to hold her wolf back so far but her control began to snap. Very seldom did she have to worry about the animal inside breaking loose but the ache in her gums warned that her teeth wanted to lengthen. She craved to bite and claim her mate.

Luckily Jace seemed to know when she reached her limit and slowly started to enter her. His cock stretched her as Jace filled her. The connection strengthened the bond between the two of them. Piper could feel the link joining them pulse in her heart.

Crying out, she clung to Jace as he withdrew gradually before plunging deep.

Mate.

The word bounced around in her head as Jace started to thrust rapidly. Piper had to clamp her teeth together to resist the overwhelming urge to sink her canines into Jace's shoulder.

Her lover was braced above her, sweat dripping down his forehead as he snapped his hips, taking her harder with each drive. Back bowed, she shuddered in pleasure. She wanted to let go. Needed to be taken and claimed.

It was getting harder and harder to stop herself from marking Jace.

"Let go," Jace told her. "Give it all to me."

He didn't know what he was asking. Couldn't understand that she was unable to comply with his request. She didn't want to turn into the monster that took her choices from her.

She wouldn't do that to Jace.

"You belong to me," Jace snarled while still pushing into her with powerful pushes. "Mine."

Bliss swamped her. A scream ripped from her throat as she finally lost all restraint. Her teeth dropped, cutting her lip. She had no control over the partial shift.

"Yes!" Jace called, losing his own battle in self-control.

Piper fell over the edge of climax hanging on to Jace to anchor herself. Jace's shout mixed with hers as they both reached satisfaction.

His heavy weight collapsed on top of her. She pressed her fingers into his strong back before stroking his muscles. He lifted his head and grinned.

Relief she hadn't bitten him mixed deep inside her with a touch of disappointment. She didn't know how long she could fight the need to mate with Jace.

"Whatever you're thinking about can wait," Jace told her, cupping her face. "Just relax."

Nodding, she closed her eyes and accepted his sweet kiss. There would time enough to worry later. She wouldn't lose this moment on what ifs. She was in Jace's arms and that was all that she needed to concentrate on. "I love you."

"I love you too."

Chapter Two

His feet pounded against the asphalt as Jace reached mile five of his morning run. The chill of the early morning air felt good against his sweat-laden flesh.

Even in the two years since he'd retired from service, he still woke up at the same time for his workout. He didn't have to stay in shape to fight for his country any longer, but it was habit.

He was glad now that he hadn't broken the routine. With the changes in his life recently, he lived in constant worry that Piper was in danger.

A werewolf. The love of his life was an actual werewolf.

It was still so unbelievable. Even though he'd known there was something in her past that scared her, the fact that she could turn into a wolf was simply amazing. If he hadn't seen it for himself, he wouldn't believe it.

But he had witnessed her transformation six months ago and almost daily since then.

Piper had revealed her true self in order to protect him. She'd killed the man that had tormented her for years, the monster who had attacked a trusting woman, changing her life in one night.

Fury still surfaced when he thought about what Piper had lived through. She didn't deserve the pain and suffering. He'd vowed early on that she would never have to deal with anything like that again.

He would keep that promise to her.

That was why he'd called in his old buddy. Mitch Bryant was someone he trusted more than anyone else in the world. At least until he'd met Piper.

Mitch would help them. The old soldier was the best he knew at ferreting out intel that Jace didn't have access to. Having spent years in the military in the same Special Forces unit as Jace, Mitch had more experience than any other members. He also had an open mind.

If Piper's secret had to be revealed to anyone, Jace was sure Mitch was the best bet and Mitch would also do anything to protect her. Mitch was just built that way.

The monitor on his wrist beeped, pulling him from his thoughts. He slowed down so that he could gradually come to a quick walk. His body hummed happily from the workout.

The house that he shared with Piper appeared ahead.

He loved their beach home. The first permanent place that he'd ever had in his life. His father had been a military man so growing up, they'd moved from base to base. As an adult he'd served his time always looking forward to the next tour. It wasn't until he'd first started to consider a retirement that he'd asked himself what he really wanted—and he wanted a home.

The move to Blue Cove had been deliberate. He was far enough from any large city that he didn't have to be surrounded constantly by people. At the same time, he was only half an hour away from his old base in San Diego.

He took the wooden porch steps two at a time. Movement out of the corner of his eye caught his attention. A young man stood about a block away in sweats, stretching out his long legs. Another runner? Normally he wouldn't question a stranger's presence but Jace hadn't heard of anyone new moving into the neighborhood. Blue Cove was a hot spot for tourists but his residence was far enough from the normal visitor attractions that seeing anyone unfamiliar concerned him.

Before Jace had a chance to really worry, though, the man took off in the opposite direction at a steady pace. Jace shook his head. He was becoming paranoid. Since he'd started looking into werewolves and how to protect Piper, he'd started to see danger everywhere.

Piper didn't know enough about what she transformed into for them to understand what was happening. It seemed that the werewolves she'd met wouldn't even consider helping her. Her years on the run had only confused her more. No one would talk with her. Piper had been unable to learn what was in store for her. He had tried to contact one couple that Piper had mentioned to him. That had been Mitch's first assignment. He'd tracked them down on what little information Piper had. Jace had called but they'd hung up on him after only a few words. When he'd tried a second time, the number had no longer been in service.

Jace hadn't pushed further.

Stepping onto the large deck outside the kitchen, Jace spotted Piper through the window. She was still dressed in a pair of loose cotton pants and his old USMC shirt. Flipping her long hair over her shoulder, she peered down into a pan on the stove with a frown.

Her attempts at cooking hadn't been very successful so far. Still, she never gave up.

He slid the patio door open quietly. Mumbling, she stirred whatever it was she was cooking. Something was burning. He could smell that for himself. A huge sigh came from her before she pulled off the pan then tossed it into the sink. Jace wrapped his arms around her from behind. She didn't even jump.

"You're getting better at listening," he complimented.

"You walk on the tips of your toes when you're trying to sneak up on me. It makes your shoes squeak."

That was a good catch. Jace couldn't hear it but they'd been experimenting with what enhancements Piper had. The fact that she could now pick up small things like that impressed him. She'd been reluctant at first to test her skills, but she was coming around.

"Plus, you smell like sweat and salt water," she added.

He turned her and saw her smiling. "Yeah? You want me to shower?"

"No." She ran her hands down his neck. "I like it."

He spun her around until his back was to the cabinet and she was in front of him. "Show me how much?"

She took a step back. She ran her gaze from his head to his feet. "Take off your shirt," she ordered.

He yanked it off and tossed it to the floor. Piper grinned before she took a step forward. She ran her nail over his nipple, causing him to arch under her touch. She caught the hard nub between her thumb and forefinger and squeezed. He reached for her but she backed away again. "Now your pants."

His cock was already hard as he slid his sweats down to his knees. He lifted one foot and removed his shoes and socks before doing the same on the other. Then he let the remaining clothes fall to the floor.

She stepped up and grasped his cock, pumping him a few times.

Pressing his mouth to hers, he was glad. With hurried hands he tugged and yanked until she was naked with him. Jace pushed Piper down to the tiled floor and entered her slowly.

He took her hard and fast out in the open and without the cushion of a bed. There were times when he just couldn't help himself. He couldn't get enough of her, wanted Piper all the time.

They came together as their soft murmurs and cries filled the room. Afterward, Jace helped Piper onto her feet, still holding onto her.

"Shower together?" he suggested.

Nodding, she swayed toward him. "Damn, you take my breath away."

"Good." He led her through the house to the master bathroom. "And after, I'll make breakfast."

She snorted. "Yeah? That's probably a good idea."

"What were you trying to make?"

"Biscuits and gravy, but the gravy was all lumpy."

So his love wasn't a culinary artist. He could live with that. Turning on the hot water, he pushed her into the stall. "How about some pancakes?"

"Fine." Piper pouted just a little.

Jace caught her bottom lip with his teeth and nibbled.

"If you keep that up, we'll go another round," she warned.

He shook his head while chuckling. He wasn't young enough to go again so soon. Although with Piper he had a better recovery time than most men his age.

Grabbing a wash cloth, he soaped it up and began to wash Piper. Her body always seemed to mold to his hands when he touched her, the softness of her curves a contrast to her toned arms and legs mesmerizing. He placed kisses on her scrubbed skin until she took the cloth from him. Piper laughed as she pumped his cock with her soapy palm.

Jace returned the favor by burying two fingers into her tight pussy. By the time they'd shut off the water and were towel drying each other his erection was bumping against her thigh.

"Food first," he said sternly.

Piper winked but stopped teasing. "Spoilsport."

He tried to grab a hold of her but she ducked away, giggling. He followed her into the bedroom. It was good to hear her laugh. They needed to talk about Mitch before his friend arrived but he hated to ruin her good mood.

Glancing at the clock on the nightstand, he noted they only had about an hour before Mitch showed.

As much as Piper would resist at first, he knew she would eventually come around. She wasn't the type of woman that would let her fear rule her. He pulled on a clean pair of jeans as Piper dressed in another pair of soft cotton pants. Her skin was more sensitive than his. He didn't know if that was because of her shifting ability or not, but he'd buy her as many comfortable fabrics as she wanted. Taking care of his partner was something that made him feel good.

"I'll start a fresh pot of coffee," she said, interpreting his thoughts.

Once again she was wearing one of his T-shirts. Damn he loved seeing her dressed in his clothes. "Okay. I'll get the batter started."

In the six months that they'd lived together, they'd found an easy rhythm that worked for them. It was the same at the bar.

Piper worked as his manager and he could trust her to run the front of the house as he devoted his time to the kitchen and orders. The day she'd come into his office to interview for the position, he'd known that she was the one for him.

Love at first sight? Fate? He didn't know. All he could say for sure was that something deep inside him had known.

She hadn't made it easy on him. Years of running had made her skittish.

He poured the pancake mix into a skillet as Piper set the butter and syrup on the island. On her way back around, she handed him a mug of coffee. He accepted the drink with a kiss.

Family. Early morning breakfast being made as they each did their part. That was what he had been searching for his entire life. Piper had given him that.

Sure there had been a sense of brotherhood between his unit, the other men that he'd shared a connection and fought beside. Deep, true, unquestioning love he received from Piper though.

"You're lost in thought this morning," she commented, as he set the platter of food between their plates.

"I know you don't want to talk about it but we need to discuss what we're going to tell Mitch."

She paused with her fork halfway to the serving dish. "Jace."

"I trust him. We need his help."

"Why?" she asked softly. "Why do we have to do anything?"

Sighing, he set his fork down. "You shouldn't have to live a half-life. Always afraid. We need to know how to protect us."

"What if we find out something worse than what we think?"

"Come here," he requested.

She rose and came around the table. Drawing her onto his lap, he cupped her face. "Then we deal with it. Not knowing isn't going to make anything easier."

"I don't want you to find out something you can't live with."

The confession tore at his heart. "Never, baby. I promise."

Instead of replying, she laid her forehead against his chest. Embracing her tightly, Jace tried to think of words to reassure her.

"I'll never give you up. You're all I've ever wanted."

She nodded.

"Let's eat."

Piper moved back to her stool.

"I think we should tell him everything," she said.

Choking, he grabbed for his coffee. The hot liquid burned his tongue but helped get the food down. "What?" he managed.

Her eyes were wide. "Sorry."

Waving that off, Jace searched her face. "You really want to tell him all of it?"

She shrugged. "Yes? I mean…if you trust him. Wouldn't he need all the facts to really help?"

Jace had considered the same thing but he was just so shocked Piper had brought it up. "It would be best."

"Then that is what we have to do."

Even though he was only halfway through with his food, he pushed his plate away.

Piper glanced up at him. "What?"

"You're amazing."

"You're just now figuring that out?" she kidded.

A squeal escaped her as he caught her around the waist and lifted her. Before Jace could do more than throw her over his shoulder, the doorbell rang.

All laughter left Piper as she tensed.

"That'll be Mitch," he said setting her back down on her feet.

"Yeah."

He dropped a kiss on the top of her head before turning to stroll out of the kitchen. He could hear Piper gathering up their dishes.

Suddenly he was nervous. He wiped his palms on his jeans as they started to sweat. He hoped he was doing the right thing. They needed information, and he trusted Mitch, but a small part of his was still terrified about how his best friend would react.

Jace reached the front door. His hand shook as he unlocked it.

Mitch was grinning when Jace opened the door. He didn't have time to brace himself before the large man jumped at him.

It was only his quick reflexes and experience with Mitch's greeting that kept him on his feet as he found himself with his arms full of six-foot-two tattooed muscle.

"Damn!" he grunted. "Did you put on weight?"

Mitch laughed loudly pounding on his back. "Nope, you've just gone soft."

Jace growled, pushing Mitch off him. He looked good. His dark blond hair was still cut short, making his large hazel eyes appear even brighter. And it looked like his buddy had gained weight. Oh, Mitch's stomach was still flat and there wasn't an ounce of fat on him, but Jace would swear the muscles in Mitch's arms and shoulders had doubled. "Get in here." He grabbed his friend, shoving him deeper into the house.

"Nice digs," Mitch commented, looking around.

Unlike Jace, Mitch was renting an apartment close to their old base. Jace wondered when Mitch would consider retiring to get his own place. Jace had tried to bring the subject up but his friend always waved away Jace's concern.

"Make yourself at home while you're here."

"Maybe you shouldn't say that. I might never leave."

Shaking his head, Jace motioned toward the kitchen. "Come on, man. Come meet Piper."

"I can't wait." Mitch grinned and slapped him on the back. "Finally get to meet the woman who claimed you."

Mitch didn't know how true the words he'd spoken were.

The kitchen had been cleaned and the island wiped down by the time the two men made it. Piper stood on the other side of the island, nervously twisting her hands together.

"Wow!" Mitch exclaimed when he entered.

Jace barked out a laugh. Of course Mitch would be taken with the large, open well-lit room. Mitch was a remarkable cook, learning early in life, and enjoyed the duty. He had always said that if he hadn't joined the military, he would be a world famous chef. Jace believed him.

When he'd retired, Jace had even tried to get Mitch to come cook at the bar. He was still working on stealing Mitch, in fact. It bothered Jace that Mitch could be sent off on a mission at any time and he would lose touch with his best friend. If Mitch was to join him at the bar, he wouldn't have to worry about his buddy as much.

Mitch turned to Piper and grinned. "Wow, again."

She blushed but smiled slightly.

"I've got to say, brother, you did real well."

He held in a moan. Mitch's sense of humor was on the dry side and not everyone knew how to handle him. Luckily he seemed to remember his manners and held out his hand to Piper.

"Mitch Bryant, darling."

Piper lifted an eyebrow but clasped her hand in his. "Piper Maxwell."

"A beautiful name for a beautiful lady."

"All right, that's enough." Jace was man enough to admit that anyone flirting with Piper irritated him.

The grin Mitch shot him told him Mitch was doing it on purpose. Piper was shaking her head as she backed away. The twitch of her lips showing her amusement as well.

He grumbled but wasn't going to give Mitch any more fun.

"Coffee?" Piper held up a pot.

"Please, the drive was longer than I thought."

While Piper fixed Mitch up with his beverage, Jace pulled out a stool. "Have a seat. We appreciate you coming."

"No problem." Mitch shrugged, and Jace knew it wasn't really an issue for him. If anyone from the unit needed him then Mitch would be the first one there.

"We have a lot to discuss but first I need a promise," Jace said, as Piper passed a cup toward him. He pushed it over to his friend. Piper had positioned herself on the other side of the counter. Far away from Mitch in case he reacted badly and close enough to the back door that she could escape if need be. Jace knew how her mind worked but he wouldn't let her run. If Mitch did cause any trouble, Jace was well trained to handle his friend.

Mitch blew on his coffee before taking a small sip. "What exactly am I promising?"

"Whatever you hear today must remain between the three of us. You can't tell anyone, ever."

It was to Mitch's credit that he didn't answer right away. As good as the man was, he knew better to vow something that he might not be able to keep.

"It's a matter of life and death," Jace added.

"Are y'all in trouble?" Mitch's back had straightened with tension.

"Not like you're thinking," Jace assured him.

Their gazes locked. Jace kept his features as calm as possible while his buddy studied him.

"I promise."

The words, spoken quietly, sent a wave of gratitude through Jace. He glanced at Piper, who was biting her bottom lip.

"Okay." Jace blew out a breath. "This is how it started." And Jace told him everything.

He started at the bar and the night that he'd found out about Piper. He didn't skim over the part where Piper had killed Joe. Instead he told the entire story of what he'd witnessed. Mitch didn't interrupt, even though Jace could see dozens of questions play across his face.

He backtracked to Piper's story and how she had been changed. It was hard to relay the torture she had experienced. She backed herself farther away from the two of them, even though Mitch never glanced at her.

His friend kept his eyes on Jace the entire time.

When he finally stopped talking, his throat was dry and he felt nauseous. Mitch remained silent for several minutes.

Piper was shaking as she watched them.

After what seemed like forever, Mitch finally stood and looked over at her. He didn't move toward her, though. Instead he dipped his head and jammed his hands in his pockets.

In a low, controlled voice Mitch spoke, "This...I've *got* to see."

Chapter Three

Piper really didn't think this was a good idea. Still she followed Jace and his friend out of the back door, down the deck steps and into the yard.

Her heart was beating furiously and she felt dizzy.

Did she really trust this stranger enough to shift in front of him? No, but she did believe in Jace, and he wanted her to do this.

Normally when she started her transformation, she'd undress first. It wasn't necessary though. She'd shifted before in her clothes and although they'd disappeared when she'd turned back, she had no trouble becoming her wolf in clothes.

She moved several feet from the two of them and dropped to her knees. She needed to calm down first or her transformation would hurt more. She closed her eyes and breathed deeply.

"Give her a little time," Jace said to Mitch.

Piper was glad that he understood how difficult this was for her. Before they'd come outside, Jace had even told her she didn't have to do this. But she did. If

Mitch was going to help them, he needed to know for certain.

Closing her eyes, she pictured her other form. She actually didn't know if that helped or not, but she'd read about shifting like that in a book and it made sense. The easiest time to shift was when she was scared. The wolf seemed to take over at that point and she was able to just let go. But her nightly runs had helped her control herself better, so she could now call on her animal to come forward anytime.

It took several moments before she felt the tingle down her spine. She lost herself in the pain and sound of limbs stretching.

When she did open her eyes, she saw the world in black and white. The fact that she couldn't see color was always a little frightening. Even with the shaded vision, though, her eyesight was sharper. Plus all of her other senses were magnified when she shifted.

"Holy shit!"

The cry scared her enough that she dropped to a defensive stance, baring her fangs as she peered up at Mitch.

His face had gone stark white. "Holy shit!" he repeated.

Jace had positioned himself between her and his friend. Piper didn't like that. If Mitch was to attack, she didn't want Jace injured.

"That is fucking amazing!"

Well that wasn't exactly fear she was hearing. Jace must have picked up on it also because his shoulders dropped some of their stiffness.

"Can I...? Can she...?"

Piper dropped to her stomach and just watched the humans.

"What?" Jace pressed.

"Can I touch her? Does she know us?"

Chuckling, Jace waved his hand. "Yeah, crouch down."

"Can you come closer, Piper?" Jace asked her.

She debated. The enjoyment she received from Jace petting her called to her but she wasn't sure if Mitch would have the same effect. She didn't want to hurt Jace's best friend.

"It's okay." Jace gestured for her get up. "I promise."

As she climbed to her feet and started toward him, she perked up her ears to catch any sounds that shouldn't be around them. Not finding anything out of the ordinary, she relaxed enough to flop down at Jace's feet. He'd know what she wanted.

If moaning was possible, she would have let out a relieved sound when Jace sat beside her, burying his hand in the fur at the base of her neck. Oh yeah, that spot was her favorite. Hard to reach on her own.

His petting drew enough of her attention that she didn't tense when Mitch moved closer. She eyed him warily as he joined them on the ground. The fact that he wasn't at her head helped resist the urge to bare her teeth, so she went completely still when he reached out and his hand hovered over her flank.

"May I?"

Well, it showed manners that he'd asked, but she couldn't actually answer him. Instead she huffed heavily.

"I think that's a yes," Jace told him with a smile.

She needed to master a glare in her wolf form. Maybe she could practice.

Mitch's palm gently brushed over her thigh and Piper found she didn't mind the touch. Laying her head on top of Jace's leg, she closed her eyes and accepted the petting.

"Not sure what to say here," Mitch spoke quietly.

She didn't know why he was whispering.

"I'm in awe though."

Thumping her tail, she tried she show her appreciation of his acceptance.

"Every time she transforms, it both astonishes and scares me. The only thing I know about what happens is from movies and books. I would have never believed this was possible. But what if someone found out about her? I have to be able to protect her."

Piper licked at Jace's hand. She knew that he worried, but for the first time, she truly understood why he was pushing her to know more about her change. Jace's mind worked differently from hers. He gathered information and made a plan. Piper was more of the 'wait and see what happens' type of person.

"We'll figure this out. I actually might know where to look."

"Really?" Jace's tone was sharp.

"Yeah, I was going through some records on our last mission."

"Wait!" Jace demanded. "Why were you looking at our assignment?"

Mitch grunted. "I always hacked into our files. Made sure the reports we gave were accurate and no one was messing with the intel."

"You're a paranoid son of a bitch," Jace told him.

"Yeah well." Mitch shrugged. "Anyway, Cody reported he saw something strange the second night on watch."

Jace frowned. "He never told me."

"Didn't say a word until later. That's suspicious right there," Mitch declared with conviction.

"I'm almost worried about what you're going to say," Jace confessed.

Piper wanted to reach up and sooth him. Instead she snuggled deeper into his lap. The new positioned blocked her view of Mitch but she would hear if he moved—especially since both men continued to run their fingers over her.

She liked the extra attention.

"What did he say?" Jace finally asked.

"About two hours after he'd gone on guard, he thought he saw someone through the trees. You remember how thick the jungle was. A lot of soldiers thought they saw things. Being alone out there causes shadows to morph and if you're not careful, you start seeing shit that doesn't exist."

While Jace had told her a little about his time in the service, he'd never shared anything like what Mitch was talking about. She couldn't imagine being so far from home, in some foreign place, scared and fighting for their life.

"Cody reported to his shrink that he swore he saw a young man staring at him through the jungle. When he started to approach, the figure moved away slowly. By the time he got to the spot, he didn't find anything but fresh paws print. Huge prints. Then he heard a howl."

The men fell silent.

Piper lifted her head. Jace was shaking his head. "He never told me."

"Hell, man," Mitch replied. "What would you have said?"

"I don't... I don't know."

"Nothing to say. He didn't say anything to us and if he had, we would have laughed it off. But now that we do know about shape-shifters — or whatever — maybe we should talk to him."

"I'll think about it," Jace said after several beats. "But we should get ready for work. Are you coming with us?"

Piper rose when Jace smacked her back lightly.

"Yeah, I could use a drink."

"I bet," Jace said with a smile. "If you wanted to get your hands dirty in the kitchen, Marcus wouldn't mind if you joined him."

"Just might do that. I'll head inside and clean up first, though."

Piper waited until Mitch had disappeared back through the house before she started to change back. By the time she was finished, her muscles ached and she was panting.

Jace took the blanket they kept on one of the chairs and wrapped her up.

"Are you going to talk to your other friend?" she asked.

"I'm not sure. Cody was only with me for only one job. I don't know him as well as Mitch. But if he mentioned what he saw to his counselor, it may be worth getting a hold of him."

"Is that why he is seeing a psychiatrist? Because he saw a werewolf?"

"No, we all have to report to a shrink when we come off a classified mission. It's part of trying to keep our heads on straight."

"Oh."

"I'll talk more about it to Mitch before we decide. I think Cody is still in, so it wouldn't be too difficult to track him down."

She snorted. "Especially if Mitch can break into all of your records."

"You're telling me. Damn, that man is one scary dude sometimes."

There was nothing else to say on that, although secretly Piper liked the fact that Mitch was a little on the crazy side. He'd accepted her easily enough. It was interesting that Jace's best friend was even more paranoid than even Jace had believed. While they were looking into Piper's problem, maybe she could find out what caused Mitch to be so suspicious.

"Can he really cook?"

"Yeah, just wait until he gets to the bar. You won't believe what that man can do in a kitchen."

* * * *

Piper couldn't put into words how good Mitch's food was. If she hadn't witnessed for herself the preparation of the masterpiece she'd been served, she would have sworn it had come from some five-star restaurant.

Mitch waved off everyone's compliments but the pleased gleam in his eye was obvious. Already she liked Mitch and that was rare for her.

Even though she had been terrified sharing her secret with someone new then shifting in front of him, Mitch somehow just made her want to spend time with him.

A group of loud college-aged guys came in, drawing Piper out of her thoughts. She had to get back to work.

She grabbed an apron and quickly tied it around her waist before heading in the direction of the young men's table where they were seating themselves. Jeers and teasing greeted her as she stepped up.

"Okay, guys." She held up her hands. "First let's see some ID and then we'll get you all taken care of."

There was some good-natured groaning but each of the six pulled out their wallets. Anderson's Loft was a popular spot for twenty and thirty year olds but they all knew that Jace ran a clean place. No underage drinking, drugs or any other illegal activities.

Piper checked to make sure all the guys were of drinking age before taking their order of beer and tequila shots. "Be right back," she told them then headed for the bar.

She was halfway across the floor when the door opened again. Glancing over her shoulder, she smiled at the newcomer. "Take a seat anywhere. I'll be right with you."

Jace smiled at her when she reached the counter. She handed over the ticket she'd written the order on. "Time to get to work, boss," she teased.

"Yes, ma'am."

Patting the dark wood top while smirking at him, she turned on her heel. There was something in air. A static connection between the two of them. It might be from her shifting earlier, the stress or maybe there was always a sort of awareness between the two. But tonight she could feel that something important was going to happen.

Of course she could just be still riding the wave of shock that Mitch knew about her. Mitch came out of the kitchen and they passed each other as she went to take the new customer order. Mitch winked at her.

It was going to be okay.

The man sitting at one of the high-top tables looked to be in his early twenties. She'd have to card him too. His light brown hair was long and shaggy but not in a stylish fashion. Piper got more of an impression that the young man had missed several haircuts.

He glanced up and her gazed locked on his brown eyes. Sad eyes.

"Hi," she greeted. "Welcome to Anderson's Loft."

"Thank you," he responded softly.

"I'm sorry but I do need to see some ID."

He bit his lip but nodded. She waited while he slowly withdrew his wallet from an inside pocket of his light jacket. Fumbling with removing a driver license from the protective sleeve, he flushed a little.

Setting the document on the table, he peered up at her. Piper slid her hand over the hard plastic and picked it up. Bobby Gibson, twenty-two, from Flagstaff, Arizona.

"Okay, sir." She offered him a small smile. "What can I get you?"

"I'll... Uh I'll have a beer, please."

"What kind?"

"Um, Bud Light?"

So not a big drinker, she hazarded. Nervous, definitely. Maybe he was meeting someone. A date. Blind date? "You got it."

She set the license back down and strolled over to the bar. She handed over the ticket for the new order then picked up the order for the large group.

After delivering the first round to the cheerful young guys, she glanced over at the lone man. He was watching her but not in a way that was creepy. Instead the stranger reminded her of a lost little boy searching for something.

Well, hell. She didn't know where that feeling had come from. She'd never been great at reading people in the first place. Jace had this uncanny ability to look at someone and just know when there was more going on. Then he'd use that intimidating but caring stare to make someone want to reveal their deepest darkest secrets.

She knew from experience.

Piper had never been able to relate to anyone other than Jace. Maybe she should have Jace serve this Bobby guy and see what Jace could pick up. But another quick peek and she knew she needed to tread carefully with the uneasy young man.

Jace slid the bottle of beer across the counter at her. She picked it up and sauntered back over to the high-top.

"Here you go," she said cheerfully, while handing over the bottle.

"Thank you." Their fingers brushed, and Piper felt the jolt.

Gasping, she jumped back crying out. *No!* No this could not be happening. Not after all this time. She was safe here. Jace had promised that no one would get to her.

The beer knocked over and spilled onto the table. Bobby Gibson jumped to his feet. "I'm sorry. I...didn't..."

"Piper." Jace's arms came around her, pulling her back into his body.

"No," she said, before a whimper escaped.

"What the hell is going on?" Jace demanded.

"I thought..." Bobby said in a harsh whisper. "I only wanted to talk to her."

If Jace hadn't been holding onto her tightly, she would have been out of the bar before anyone could catch her.

"I'll go," Bobby said quickly before he turned to leave.

"Hey there!" Mitch caught Bobby's arm. "Slow down, buddy. We'll not hurt you."

Bobby looked horrified at being stopped by Mitch.

"Let's go to the office," Jace said.

Mitch nodded and propelled Bobby forward.

Piper couldn't move her feet. She clung to Jace, needing his solid, strong presence.

"What is it? What is going on?"

Piper couldn't control the shakes that took over her body.

"Oh, baby." He gathered her closer and half pulled, half carried her away from the scene she was making in the middle of the bar.

Embarrassment would hit her later. Right then all she wanted was for Jace to continue to hold her.

"Brittany, I need you to watch the front," Jace ordered the waitress.

"You got it, boss."

Piper couldn't even look at Brittany.

Why was this happening now? Just when she'd thought that they would be able to figure everything out. She'd trusted Mitch with her secret and all of a sudden this had happened!

Jace led her through the short hall to stop in front of his closed office door. "Tell me," Jace encouraged cupping her face. "What is it?"

Piper peered up at Jace. "He's like me," she managed.

Chapter Four

Jace would do anything in his power to protect Piper. He knew it wasn't actually possible to guard her from every bad experience in the world but damn it, he wanted to.

She was still trembling when he led her into his office. Mitch glanced up at him with a worried look on his face. The kid was sitting on the couch with his face buried in his hands. He cringed when Jace and Piper entered.

Encouraging Piper to the desk chair, Jace watched the young man carefully. He too was shaking and although Jace was unhappy about the result the stranger's visit was having on Piper, he found himself more than curious about this stranger.

"What's your name?" Jace asked after Piper was seated behind him. There was no way this guy would be able to hurt Piper before Jace got to him.

Mitch was also standing, legs braced apart with his arms crossed over his chest, next to the kid.

"Bobby Gibson. Look I'm sorry. They told me where to come and I thought... I'll leave, I promise! Just please don't hurt me."

"We're not going to hurt you. Who told you to come here?"

"I met a couple about a month ago. I knew they were like me but when I approached them, the guy attacked. After I managed to get free, they told me to leave town."

Jace glanced back at Piper. She nodded. They both knew that she'd had a very similar interaction a few years before. The same couple that Jace had tried to contact.

"I tried to ask questions but they wouldn't even listen. Then the woman told me if I really wanted someone to talk to, there was this guy in California that kept calling them. They gave me your name, Jace, and that led me here."

Jace scratched his chin. If everything Bobby was telling them was true, this kid needed their help. And maybe they'd be able to learn more too. "Why did you come here?"

Bobby's dark brown gaze bore into his. "I didn't have anywhere else to go."

Behind him Piper made a sound. He whirled around and saw tears pooling in her eyes that had not yet fallen. She felt for the young man. That much was obvious. Hopefully she would be okay with helping the kid because Jace couldn't just let him walk out on his own.

He made eye contact with Mitch and inclined his head toward Bobby so that he would continue to watch him before sinking to his knees in front of Piper.

"You okay?"

Nodding, she gripped his hands. "I believe him," she whispered.

"Me too. But we still have to be careful." He gave her hand a quick squeeze before standing back up.

"Please relax." Jace smiled at the younger guy. "My name is Jace, and this is my friend Mitch. Behind me is Piper."

"I know. I've…uh, been watching you."

Narrowing his eyes, Jace remembered where he'd seen Bobby before. "My morning run."

Bobby flushed. "Yeah, I wasn't entirely sure why that couple would send me to you when they obviously wanted nothing to do with me. I just wanted to check you out before I approached."

"You've never come inside the bar before."

"No, I've just been watching." Bobby glanced in Mitch's direction before dropping his gaze back down. "I don't know why I came in tonight. I just wanted to talk to her."

Her meaning Piper. If Bobby had been watching them at both the house and bar then he had to know they were together. Somehow, though, Jace didn't believe that Bobby was interested in Piper sexually. It might just be his gut but Bobby's pull toward Piper had to do with them both being werewolves.

"Why did you want to talk to me?"

Piper's soft question surprised Jace. She didn't move from her half hidden place behind him but that seemed okay with Bobby, since he relaxed a little into the back of the couch.

"You seemed so happy. Like I said, I've been watching you and I just wanted to know how you deal with it. Does it get any better? This thing that we can turn into?"

Before Piper could answer, Jace interrupted, "How did you know she was the one that could shift?"

Licking his bottom lip, Bobby looked up at Jace. "I saw her."

That wasn't good. How long exactly had Bobby been watching them?

"It was only once. This afternoon. And it was so amazing to see her shift and then the two of you just sitting with her. When I got here I wasn't sure… That couple almost hurt me and I didn't want to go through that again. But today, seeing you three, it was truly wonderful. I just had to try."

The pure longing in Bobby's voice tugged at Jace's heartstrings. "How long have you been able to transform?" Jace asked him.

Bobby stiffened and paled.

"Hey." Mitch walked over to the couch. "Just stay calm. We're not going to turn on you. Why don't I grab us some coffee?"

"That's a good idea," Jace agreed. They needed to have Bobby comfortable around them. Trust would hopefully come in time, so the best they could hope for was keeping Bobby from leaving.

While Mitch left the room, Jace turned to make sure Piper was handling everything okay. He shouldn't have worried. Even if she'd had a moment of panic, Piper was strong and brave. Color returned to her face and she was just as beautiful as ever.

She smiled at him, letting him know she was doing all right.

"Here we go," Mitch announced as he returned with a carafe of coffee and four mugs. He also had small containers of sugar and cream. "Marcus was already ahead of our thinking and had this all ready for us."

Piper stood and pushed the chair across from Bobby. Mitch passed out mugs and poured coffee. Piper sat back down while Jace sat on the arm on her seat. Bobby stiffened when Mitch joined him on the couch but since Mitch remained close to his own side, Bobby seemed to relax a little.

"Can you tell us how you became…this way?" Piper asked gently.

Nodding, Bobby peered at her. "I'll try." His hand was shaking when he set his cup down.

"Take your time," Jace encouraged. "I know it's not easy. You don't know us, but if you have been observing us then hopefully you know we're good people."

"Yes, I think so," Bobby consented. "That's why I came in here. And I didn't want to disturb you at your house. I tried to talk to you this morning but I lost my nerve."

Poor kid. So alone and wounded. He reminded Jace of Piper when they'd first met.

"Just tell us what you're comfortable sharing." Jace hoped his calm tome would settle Bobby.

Bobby took a deep breath before blowing it out slowly. "My family is from Tucson. When I got accepted into the University of Arizona, I was so happy to get to remain close to them. Plus the university has an awesome life science program. I just got my bachelor degree and was accepted into a program to go for my master's. My parents were so proud they arranged for the three of us to come to California."

As Bobby spoke, Jace could pick up the affection he had for his parents.

"We had just hit the state line when my dad pulled into an old rest stop. My mom had needed to use the bathroom and we all wanted to stretch out legs." Bobby's voice dropped. "The place was deserted but clean."

A bad feeling settled in Jace's stomach. Piper gripped his hand.

"My dad walked my mom over to the women's restroom and I went off in the other direction. I don't really know how far I walked. I was just sort of zoned out after the long drive. Then I heard them start screaming."

Bobby shuddered, and Mitch moved closer patting his shoulder. "Take a deep breath," Mitch told Bobby. "That's right, good, just like that."

While Bobby breathed in and out, Jace glanced at Piper. Her gaze was on the kid and sympathy swam in her eyes.

Jace was pretty sure they all knew what had happened to Bobby's parents—and to him.

"I'm okay," Bobby said shakily. "I started to run back toward my mom and dad. When I reached the walkway, I couldn't hear my mother anymore but my dad was yelling for me to run. I couldn't though. I had to see."

He gulped. "Blood was everywhere and there were two…monsters standing over my parents. My dad wasn't making a sound anymore. His throat was ripped open."

"Oh, honey," Piper said softly.

Tears had filled Bobby's eyes and a few drops fell. "I turned but before I could even take a step one of those things was on me. I just remember the pain. Great pain as it tore at my back. I must have blacked out. When I woke again, I was in the back of my parents' SUV and there were two strangers with me. One drove while the other kept watching me."

Wiping his eyes, Bobby shook his head. "I didn't understand what was happening. At first I thought maybe they found me and were going to take me to the hospital."

"How long did they have you?" Piper asked.

"I think a week. I was pretty out of it but I know I was with my parents on the fifth and when I finally got away, it was the twelfth."

"They made you drink their blood?" Piper guessed.

"Yeah, I couldn't fight them off. After the first couple of times I started to feel different. The first time I…I…changed, it hurt so bad I thought I was going to die."

Jace had heard the same words from Piper. He clenched his free hand. God, why did these two have to suffer? "How'd you get away?"

Bobby laughed harshly. "They left the motel door unlocked. I guess they thought I was so out of it, or maybe they didn't think I could run. But they left late one night. They had been talking about going to a bar and I pretended to be asleep. After they left, I waited ten minutes. It was the hardest thing I had to do. Lay there and wonder if they would come back right away. When I thought they had left for sure, I pulled myself off the bed and just ran."

"You're lucky to be alive," Mitch told him.

"Am I, though? After what I turn into?" Bobby asked.

"You are," Piper assured. "You're a survivor and now you're not alone anymore."

"You won't…run me out of town too?"

"No," Jace told Bobby sincerely. "At least for now, I think there is safety in numbers."

Bobby eyes were huge as his gaze met Jace's. "Thank you."

****

Piper felt wiped out from everything that had transpired over the night. Jace unlocked the front door, and she slipped inside their home. Mitch was behind them as the three of them returned home.

She was glad that Marcus and Brittany had agreed to lock up, since she just wasn't certain she would be able to remain standing much longer. After listening to Bobby's story, she couldn't get the picture of Bobby's traumatic experience from her mind. The attack and horror that had happened to the young man was even worse than hers. She'd always had to take a little responsibility for what had happened to her. She'd taken Joe home. Her first one-night stand and she had paid dearly.

Bobby had just been an innocent kid heading for a vacation with his family. He'd lost so much that night, more than anyone could truly understand. To see his family slaughtered then turn into the same thing that had murdered them would have been unthinkable.

Yet Bobby still appeared to be a sweet, innocent kid, scared and unsure about the world he'd been thrown into.

She knew Jace hadn't wanted Bobby to go back to his hotel room by himself but she wasn't sure what else they could do. Would having Bobby close by bring out her animal side more? She hoped not, since she really wanted to help him. After Bobby had admitted to being drawn to her, Piper had to admit that there was something that pulled her right back to the kid. A wave of protectiveness that was so strong she'd even gotten a little angry that Jace had been pushing him on his story.

It was so unlike her that she feared that it was a result of being so close to another shifter.

"How about we sit in the hot tub?" Jace suggested, running his hand down her back.

Soaking her body sounded like the best idea she'd heard in years. She nodded.

"How about it, Mitch?" Jace asked his friend.

"If you don't mind, I think I'll go ahead and turn in. It's been a long day and I have a feeling the next few are going to be just as exciting."

"Yeah, man. We understand," Jace assured him.

Piper was a little relieved that she would have time with just Jace. There was no doubt that the immediate future was going to be full of change, like Mitch had said. A little time in Jace's arms would go a long way to calming her.

"Why don't you get the Jacuzzi ready and I'll be right there after I lock up."

Offering Mitch a quiet goodnight before cutting through the kitchen and out onto the back deck, she blanked all the worries trying to surface.

Steps silent in the late night, Piper strolled to the corner where the hot tub was located. Hitting the button to turn on the jets, she was already feeling the peace wash over her. She was just reaching to remove the thick heavy cover when she heard Jace join her on the deck.

He wasn't trying to quiet his steps, so she expected him as he drew closer.

Stream rose as she revealed the bubbling water. She sighed, looking forward to relaxing back as his strong arms came around her. Turning in his embrace, she lifted her face for a kiss. His tongue lapped at her bottom lip so she opened and granted him access. When he ran his hands down her back to caress her ass, Piper moaned.

"Let's get these clothes off," Jace said, tugging at her T-shirt.

She started to pull the garment over her head before she realized what she was doing. "We can't do this here," she protested.

Jace finished taking her shirt off. "Relax. Mitch already headed to the guest room. He promised not to come out until morning to give us time alone."

Since the Jacuzzi was situated in the corner with three walls blocking the view, she knew no one could see them from the yard, but what if Mitch wanted a bottle of water or something?

"I see you need some convincing," Jace told her.

Piper smirked at him. She had no doubt that Jace could talk her into anything. But if she really opposed, he would understand. The question was, did she even want to resist him?

"Remember last time we soaked together?" he asked, stepping closer.

The weekend before, they'd cuddled together drinking wine. She'd ended up bent over the lip of the hot tub with

Jace taking her from behind. Just remembering that had Piper's heart speeding up.

"Oh yeah, you've not forgotten."

She let him bring her against him, no longer even considering saying no. Jace undressed her slowly before nudging her to the water. "Climb in."

She walked up the three steps and climbed into the hot water. "Oh God," she said with pleasure, sinking to her chin.

Jace's quiet laugh caught her attention. He'd removed his own clothes and was standing by the side. Already erect, Jace's cock was hard and leaking pre-cum. Piper shifted enough to reach Jace and grasp him. He hummed as he moved his hips slightly and she pumped his cock.

He was just so damn handsome. She didn't know if she would ever really get used to someone like Jace wanting her. Moving to her knees, she bent over the side and lowered her mouth to lick at the tip of his cock, tasting the salty essence.

"Suck me, baby," he pleaded.

She would, but he deserved just a little taste of his own medicine. Instead of taking him down her throat, she tongued against the veins under the tip.

Jace buried his hands in her hair but didn't force her to take more. He let her tease his shaft, making him even harder.

Only when he started trembling did she finally engulf his cock. Jace's groan was low and full of pleasure. Hollowing her cheeks, she sucked him deeply.

"Just like that." His voice had dropped and was laced with husky need.

She wanted to push him over the edge. To have him come in her mouth. The little taste of his seed she was getting wasn't enough.

With her left hand around the base of his cock she lowered her right to finger herself. Burying two fingers into her pussy, she tried to match her own pleasure with his.

"Stop."

She whimpered when Jace tugged her hair to make her release him.

"I want inside you," he told her. He climbed in the water and grasped her around the waist. "Climb on my lap."

Hurrying to comply, she straddled Jace so his cock rubbed against her mound. He teased the tip between her folds, and Piper thought she might go insane. She needed him so badly.

"Now." With his hands gripping her hips tightly, he helped lower her down.

As he began to fill her, Piper felt the bond between them sizzle.

Piper dropped her head back and just let the bliss take over her. Jace's fingers dug into her as he thrust up in powerful strokes. She didn't have to do anything, only trust that Jace would bring her the most amazing sensations of ecstasy.

"That's it," he whispered. "Give yourself over to me."

She knew she could, too. Jace would always take care of her. Give her exactly what she needed. "Love," she gasped. "Love you."

"Love you back. You're mine. All mine," he said, plunging faster.

Her breath caught and she finally flew past and over the edge. She cried out, clinging to him in climax.

She couldn't make out what Jace was saying but soon he joined her and reached completion.

Panting, she collapsed against his chest. "Mmm, I needed that."

He kissed her temple. "Me too."

Knowing she wasn't going to be moving anytime soon, she rested her head on his shoulder and peered up at him. "It's going to be okay, right?"

"I really do think so," he answered, and she could hear the honesty in his voice. "The kid needs someone and I got a good vibe from him."

"Me, too," she agreed. "I felt terrible when he told us his story."

"He's been through a lot. I think we can help him accept the animal."

Since that was what she wanted, she settled more securely against him, pleased they were on the same page. She hoped they weren't making a mistake accepting Bobby into their lives.

Only time would tell, but she felt sure that they were doing the right thing.

"Mitch is going to check him out in the morning, just to make sure."

She nodded. That would have to be enough for now.

Chapter Five

Jace wasn't surprised to see Mitch already awake and sitting at the kitchen table with a cup of coffee and his laptop. Since his friend didn't even glance up when Jace entered in, he walked around the table to peer over Mitch's shoulder.

Robert 'Bobby' Gibson's picture and information was on the screen.

"From what I've found, I'd say the kid is telling the truth. There is a police report on the attack at the rest stop. Although, the authorities blamed the violence on a group of wild animals," Mitch said without looking up.

"Well, I didn't really expect them to say the incident was orchestrated by a werewolf."

"Bobby's story sounds a lot like Piper's. I wonder how many others are out there."

"I have no idea," Jace replied. "Piper hasn't even met a handful."

"The only thing I can't figure out is why Bobby was taken. They'd kept him for five days, drank from him, fed him their blood, and then just disappeared?"

"You think they are looking for him?" Jace asked. He had the same fear.

"You said that after Piper got away from the man who changed her, he still came after her. I don't see why these two would be any different."

"And if they do come for him, they'll find Piper."

Mitch nodded. "Yeah, but I don't feel right sending Bobby out on his own, even if he does bring trouble. He's so...young. It makes me wonder if that was how I appeared before I joined the Marine Corps."

"I know." Jace didn't think he had ever been as innocent as Bobby seemed, though. "I want to help him but I have to put Piper first. I'm not even sure where to go from here."

"I want to talk to Cody. He mentioned his sighting for a reason. He believes he saw something, at least enough for it to bother him. I've gone through a lot of classified reports so far but haven't found anything as directly connected as what Cody reported."

"You know, if you keep hacking into the government's files, they are going to catch you one day."

Mitch's smile was blinding. "Let them try."

Shaking his head, Jace just slapped his buddy on the back then walked over to the coffee pot. "Call Cody. See if he'll meet."

"You got it." Mitch nodded before picking up his cell phone. "I have to admit I never thought I'd be involved in something so..."

"Weird?" Jace offered. He pulled down a large mug and poured himself a full cup.

"Cool!" Mitch corrected with a smile. "Can you imagine being able to turn into an animal? A powerful wolf or something else? Hey, what else is there?"

Jace laughed. He wasn't actually surprised that Mitch had reacted so positively. That was one of the reasons he'd chosen to share Piper's secret with him. Every time that Piper shifted and he spent any time with her in her shifted form, he felt an instant pull toward her. The bond that had been so strong from the beginning just grew every day.

Realizing Mitch was talking to him, he shook his thoughts away. "What?"

"Are there other animals to shift into? Or is it a wolf thing?"

Taking a small sip since the brew was still burning hot, he thought about Mitch's question. "Piper and I have talked about it. We're not sure. This mystical creature that I see isn't the same as what she feels. I mean... How can it even be possible? I just don't know. But if she can shift into a wolf, why couldn't someone else transform into something different?"

"Does she consider herself a werewolf or a shifter?"

"A werewolf, I guess," Piper said as she entered the kitchen. "Or that's what I've always called it. I guess it's something to think on."

She looked adorable in her torn jeans and faded gray shirt. Her long hair was pulled back with her face freshly washed and glowing. He'd been worried that all the stress of the day before would keep her in bed most of the morning. He was pleased to see her awake and seemingly happy.

"Why?" Mitch asked.

"From what I've read—which I'll admit is mostly fiction books—a werewolf is part animal and part human. As a shifter, the wolf inside is separate from the human. I don't feel like there is something inside me. It's more"—she walked to Jace—"a part of me."

Mitch was nodding. "Okay, so I wonder if it is the same for Bobby."

"He should be here soon," Piper offered. "He just called my cell and asked if he could come over. I don't think he likes being alone."

"That's good," Jace said, and offered his mug to Piper.

She kissed him lightly before accepting the coffee. That small gesture was enough to get Jace's pulse quickening. Turning, he grabbed another cup to pour himself more while running his free hand down her back, since he couldn't whisk her away right then.

"Let me call Cody real quick before Bobby gets here. Hopefully Bobby will agree to come with us."

As his friend stood and headed out to the back deck, Jace turned to Piper. "You doing okay?"

She smiled brightly. "I am. I actually feel great. I had a dream last night and it sort of settled everything inside me."

Curious, Jace leaned against the counter. "Yeah?"

"If I didn't think it was impossible, I would swear that my wolf side was talking to me. It was like that part of me was telling me that I need to protect Bobby. That he is ours. Same with Mitch. A kind of family."

Jace tried to hide his shock. Piper never talked like this. Not that there was anything wrong with her accepting the other two men, but Piper had always been a loner. It had taken him months to get through the walls she'd built.

Thinking about what she'd said, Jace ran her words around in his head. "Maybe that's what happened?" he offered.

"Huh?" Piper lowered the cup she'd just brought to her lips.

"Maybe your wolf part was actually talking to you."

"That's crazy," she said softly, although she didn't sound convinced either.

"Is it?" he asked. "You can turn into a wolf."

"Well, yeah…"

"But you don't think it's possible to have your other half contact you in dreams?"

Piper shook her head but started laughing quietly. Jace tugged her closer by her belt loops.

"It doesn't matter if it really was your wolf or not. If you're feeling good about Bobby and Mitch then I think we're on the right track. Maybe this is what we've been waiting for."

She bit her bottom lip while she ran her hands up and down his stomach. "Do you think…?"

"What?" he asked when she didn't continue.

"Was it Bobby here that was making me feel so weird lately? Is it possible my wolf side knew?"

"I don't know." Jace hugged her tight. "I wish I had all the answers for you."

"I know," she said as she rubbed her cheek against his chest. "I know."

* * * *

Piper wasn't certain if it was the best idea to show Bobby her private spot close to the beach that she shifted in. He'd already seen her in the yard but Piper just felt like she should change forms away from Jace and Mitch.

The strange over-protective feeling she'd started to have about Bobby still beat inside her and she wanted Bobby comfortable. So, even though she wasn't sure about revealing another secret to anyone, she would take Bobby to shift where she did.

When Bobby had confessed that he hated to shift and avoided it at all costs, she had known what she needed to do. After all, she had felt the very same way and it had only been with Jace's support that she'd started to accept what she was. She wanted to be able to offer that same encouragement to Bobby. And she knew he wouldn't be comfortable at the house with the two other men close by. Jace and Mitch would join them later somewhere on the beach.

When they reached the secluded clearing, Piper stopped. Bobby was practically bouncing on his toes in either nervousness or anxiety. She wasn't sure.

She turned to him. "Are you ready?"

"You're sure about this? What if I attack someone?"

"There is no one around but us. Jace and Mitch are still at the house and this is a private beach. It'll be okay."

Since Bobby didn't look convinced, Piper took his hand. The jolt wasn't the same as the reaction she got from touching Jace. Instead of the shot of love and arousal she felt for Jace, her sensation from Bobby was one of warmth and affection.

Bobby's eyes widened before he smiled brightly. "Wow."

Agreeing, she squeezed his hand. It was nice to have a connection with someone again. She loved Jace but she could feel herself growing more fond of Bobby as well, like a little brother. "It took me a long time to actually want to shift. But the more I do, the better each time feels. It's like the old saying, practice makes perfect. It even hurts less." She paused. "I think… Maybe I just don't notice as much."

Nodding, he took a deep breath. "I've never…changed on purpose."

"That's okay. I'll walk you through it. I'll be here every step of the way," she assured him.

"Okay." He stepped back. "Okay, I'll try."

Pride had her grinning at the young man. Bobby would have to fight his demons his own way. She knew that better than anyone. Hopefully, understanding his new self would help his healing process.

If anyone had told her a week ago she would be volunteering to help someone with a transformation, she would have laughed at them, especially since she was in no way an expert. She was still trying to figure things out for herself, but it just felt so natural to lead Bobby into his new life.

"Take deep breaths, calm your mind and don't be afraid," she told him softly.

He closed his eyes. That was good. Smart. His chest rose and fell with each breath.

"Find that part of yourself. Just under the surface," she said. "That part of you that wants to let you." She closed her own eyes and followed her words.

Easily she could feel the animal that was a part of her, ready and excited.

"Can you feel him?" she asked Bobby.

"Yes." His voice was low, scared.

"Remember, he won't hurt you. He *is* you."

"Should I...? What do I do?" Bobby sounded panicked.

"Breathe, just breathe. It's okay. I'm right here." To prove her words, she glided closer to him. "Don't push him away. Let him come to you. It'll feel like two pieces of a puzzle clicking together."

Her wolf was getting agitated and wanted to start the transformation. She kept a barrier between the two of them. Bobby had to shift first.

"Pull your shirt off. Accept yourself."

He didn't have to undress but it was easier and Bobby needed to prove to himself that he wanted to shift. Piper didn't open her eyes but could pick up his movements. "Good. When you're ready, take off the rest of your clothes. Just keep breathing."

It was several minutes until she could hear Bobby finally stripping off the rest of his clothes.

"Drop down. I'm right with you. Just stay calm." She removed her own outfit and fell to her hands and knees. "Connect, don't be afraid."

Bobby groaned in pain as his bones cracked and his body reshaped. She let her own wolf close to the surface and started her own change.

God, it was painful but she panted through the hurt. Shuddering before dropping down onto her stomach, she just had to catch her breath. She hadn't been lying to Bobby when she'd said that it was better for her now. She couldn't imagine how he was feeling.

When she blinked her eyes open, she could see the end of Bobby's transformation.

He was on his side, wheezing and shaking.

Climbing to her feet, she stretched just as Bobby opened his eyes, staring at her. She wished she could tell him it was okay. He was okay. Instead she slowly made her way over to him.

He tensed but she didn't stop. As soon as she was close enough, she nuzzled his neck. It was like a switch flipped in him. Suddenly he relaxed, falling back to the damp grass. Pleased with his acceptance, she continued to rub her nose against him. Bobby rolled to his back with his feet up as she continued down his stomach. He was submitting to her and she wanted to howl in approval. What an experience. Not able to stop herself from checking him over, she made certain he was fully recovered from the transformation before letting up on her touch.

Once she was sure he was okay, she butted his side, wanting him on his feet. He huffed but rolled over. Backing away, she gave him time to get comfortable on all four feet.

His first steps were hesitant but eventually he gained in confidence. She backed up a few steps before running forward and bumping against him. Bobby scrambled away. She did it again. Then one more time. On the fourth pass, Bobby dropped to a crouch and took the hit, rolling with her.

Piper licked him before launching up and withdrawing again. Bobby took the opportunity of her retreat to come at her. It was so much fun! Never before had she been able to share the playfulness she felt while in her other form. They wrestled and rolled for so long that she had to stop and catch her breath. Bobby collapsed down beside her with his tongue hanging out.

Instinct had just taken over on having another wolf with her and she had to admit, she'd never enjoyed shifting so much. Wanting to extend the joy, she nipped at Bobby's side before jumping up and running. She ran out of the clearing and down toward the beach, his heavy paws close behind.

The air was cool as they raced to the sand. She leaped cleanly over a small stump and chanced a glance back. Bobby was almost on her. Surprising, since he was smaller than she. In their human bodies he was a good several inches taller but as wolves, she towered over him. She hadn't expected that. Maybe it was because she was older? There was no telling how or why. And she didn't want to think too much on it right then. It was time to just enjoy the freedom.

Since she knew the area so well, she had a pretty good idea where Jace and Mitch would end up. Jace had told her where he and Mitch would meet them, so she quickly darted right, changing direction and glancing back to make sure Bobby remained close. It took a few feet for him to follow but when he did, he also picked up his speed. She knew an instant before he jumped her that he would.

They rolled over the loose sand. Using his momentum, Piper ended up on top of Bobby. There was no doubt that he was having as much fun as she was. His tail thumped happily as she crouched over him.

When he lifted his nose and ran it under her chin, contentment filled her. She crawled over his body before lying down next to him. He snuggled into her and she closed her eyes. They would just rest for a little bit.

Never really falling asleep, she lightly rested but remained tuned into her surroundings. She would have liked to nap like Bobby was beside her but her wolf stayed alert and ready to protect Bobby if need be. It was so quiet in their little sand bank that she couldn't find any sign of danger. Still she remained prepared.

By the time Bobby started to rouse, Piper was more than ready to run again. She let him stretch and shake before climbing back onto her paws. This time it was Bobby who took the chance and raced ahead. She had to work to keep up with his speed.

They crisscrossed across the open sand and close to the water.

When she caught the scent of Jace close by, she guided Bobby in that direction. He easily fell behind her, letting her take over their journey. Piper followed the familiar and amazing scent of Jace. She also picked up Mitch's scent mixed with her lover's. It was simple enough to track down the two men. Their location was closer to the woods than the beach.

"Ah here they are," Jace said when she led Bobby to the secluded wooded area Jace had found. It wasn't one of their usual meet up sites.

As Jace dropped to his knees, Piper rubbed against him. He chuckled, falling back and wrapping his arms around her. Now this was different. Just the feel of Jace's hands on hers was so incredible.

Settling herself on Jace's lap, she looked over at Bobby, who remained just at the opening from where they'd entered.

Licking Jace's chin then glancing back to Bobby, she hoped Jace knew what she wanted.

"Bobby," he called softly. "Can you come join us?"

Relieved that he had understood, she relaxed into Jace. Mitch sat close beside Jace, giving Bobby time to decide.

He was slow but he did eventually make his way over to them.

"If it's okay, I would like to pet you," Mitch said quietly to Bobby.

Bobby's gaze met hers and she nodded. It would be good for Bobby to get used to being touched as a wolf. She'd always been so scared for hurting Jace while in her shifted form, so it would make sense if Bobby felt the same way. Having Jace's hands on her while in her other form had helped her get over that fear. Hopefully Mitch would be able to do the same for Bobby.

Cautiously Bobby lowered to the ground and scooted forward. Piper watched closely, making sure he really was okay.

Mitch allowed Bobby to settle before he lifted his hands in the air. Just as carefully, he reached out and very gently laid his palms on Bobby's side. Bobby flinched, but when Mitch froze, Bobby seemed to understand he wasn't going to be hurt.

Jace ran his fingers through the thick fur of her side without saying a word. Just lightly petting her while Bobby got used to accepting Mitch's touch. Eventually Bobby calmed enough for Mitch to progress closer and run his hands over the small wolf. Piper let her eyes close as all was right in the world. No worry or stress. Their little group was safe.

* * * *

She must have dozed off because she woke with Jace gently shaking her. She huffed and stretched before opening her eyes and peering around. Bobby was lying across Mitch's legs as the big man continued to rub his belly.

They both looked very at ease in their position.

"Are you ready to shift back so we can eat some lunch?" Jace asked.

She was hungry and knew that Jace planned to have a barbeque. She stood and nudged Bobby to join her. Bobby happily trotted behind her as she took him back to where they'd left their clothes. Jace and Mitch followed behind at a slower pace.

It didn't take long for them to return to the clearing. Hopefully Bobby would follow her lead to transform but if not, she could change first then talk him though the process.

When she dropped to the ground, Bobby copied her. That was good. It looked like he was going to try.

Closing her eyes, she let her body take over and gave herself to the conversion. Her arms and legs were still quivering when she was done.

She pushed the hair away from her face and skimmed her gaze over Bobby as he returned to human form. "You okay?"

He nodded. Slowly she rose. Bobby was rocking back and forth.

"Bobby?"

He looked up at her and rolled her shoulders. On his knees, he clasped his hands behind him and lowered his head. "Thank you. I'll follow you anywhere, my Alpha, my leader.

Shocked she stepped back. "What?"

He lifted his head and stared right at her. "My Alpha."

"You... You can't say that," she told him sternly.

Bobby cocked his head to the side. "Why not?"

Why not? She didn't know how to answer him, he just couldn't... Taking a deep breath, she grasped his hand. "I'm sorry. I shouldn't have reacted like that."

"It's okay." He shrugged. "I'm sorry I upset you."

"No, no just don't be saying things like that."

"Sure," he agreed.

"Come on. We should head to the house." She led Bobby away, hoping that he'd drop the subject.

"Piper?" Bobby paused, and she had no choice but to turn around. "It just felt right. Like I needed to acknowledge you."

That's what bothered her. She'd woken up knowing that Bobby belonged to her. In a different way from how Jace was hers, but still Bobby was her responsibility. From all the research Jace had done over the last several months, she'd read several articles about wolves having Alphas.

The most troubling thing about what Bobby had called her was that the connection that had formed between the two of them was peaceful. Which scared the crap out of her. As if the animal part of her had just been waiting for it. If that didn't make her even more of a freak then she didn't know what else would.

Jace had more than enough to worry about. There was no way she could tell him that something was changing inside her.

Chapter Six

Jace wasn't sure what had happened after Piper and Bobby had changed back to their human form. By the time he and Mitch had gotten to the clearing, Piper had been gaping at Bobby, her face pale.

Bobby didn't say anything but his eyes remained on Piper for the entire walk back to the house. As they arrived, he was about to confront Bobby when Piper gripped his hand, holding on tight.

"How was it?" Mitch asked Bobby, cutting though the tension between them.

"I don't know. On one hand it was fantastic but on the other, it terrifies me."

"That's about how I feel. The more I shift, the better confidence I have. I feel more in control, less likely to do something wrong," Piper said.

"You'd never hurt anyone," Jace assured her. "Either of you. I think the more times Bobby can transform with Piper, the better it will be."

"Why? How can I really help him?" She waved a hand at Bobby then herself.

Jace glanced at Bobby before giving his attention back to Piper. "What is it? What's wrong?"

"I don't know what I'm doing! What if I hurt Bobby?" she cried.

"No, you could never do anything to hurt Bobby. It isn't in you to do so."

"I trust you, Piper," Bobby said.

"Maybe you shouldn't," Piper whispered.

"I don't know why you're so upset." Jace held her tight. "What can I do to help?" He had to find a way to take the worry and grief from her. The morning had started so well and he'd been excited to see what Piper and Bobby could accomplish together. He'd been so pleased sitting and petting them. "What can I do?" he repeated.

"I don't know. Everything is happening so fast. I want to protect Bobby and it kills me to think that I might end up harming him"

Now that sounded like Piper. "We'll be here to help you—Mitch and I. You don't have to do this on your own."

"We'll figure all this out," Mitch added.

Spinning around Piper faced Mitch. "How?"

"By telling me everything you know and feel. What you suspect. I'll work my fingers to the bone to get you answers. You trust Jace and now I just need you to have the same faith in me."

Piper's nose scrunched up. Jace stayed quiet, trying to see how she'd respond. "I do trust you," she confessed. "God help me, I'm pulling all of you down this rabbit hole with me but we'll go together."

"There's nowhere else I would rather be," Jace told her.

"Sounds good to me," Mitch agreed.

"I'll follow you anywhere," Bobby said quietly.

Jace stared at Bobby after his admission. If he wasn't mistaken, there was awe and a little hero worship in Bobby's tone. Jace had seen it plenty in soldiers returning home after being rescued.

"Trust your instincts for now," Jace told both Piper and Bobby. "I think that's the best we can hope for."

"I just hope it's enough," Piper murmured.

"You were changed before him, you're older, have more experience and I think just naturally more of a leader. Bobby following your lead just makes sense," Mitch said.

Piper's mouth dropped open as she paled. Jace really did not understand where the sudden bout of stress was coming from.

"It makes sense to me when he puts it that way," Bobby admitted.

Jace stepped away, pulling Piper with him. "Do you want to talk about what else is bothering you?"

She was already shaking her head before he'd finished.

Mitch's cell phone rang, drawing Jace's attention back over to him. Mitch dragged the small phone out of his pocket and smiled. "It's Cody, calling back finally."

Jace waved him off. "Go. I'll start the grill."

Mitch nodded then walked away down the steps before he answered with a friendly hello.

"Why don't you two relax at the table and I'll get lunch started," Jace suggested.

It was cute the way Bobby looked to Piper. When she gave Jace a thankful smile before turning toward the lounge chairs, Bobby followed right on her heels. He had to hold in a laugh. *Like a puppy.*

Neither Piper nor Bobby would probably appreciate that observation, so he kept it to himself. As he strolled into the kitchen, he thought about everything they'd just discussed. He hated to think that Piper was hiding something from him. His gut was telling him that she wasn't in danger but something big was on her mind. He'd do his best to give her the time she needed. But if Piper didn't figure things out for herself, he was going to step in, even if she ended up handing him his ass for his trouble.

Amused with himself, he pulled out the platter of burgers Mitch had prepared after Piper and Bobby had left to shift. Mitch wouldn't actually say what the secret ingredient he'd used was but Jace had always loved Mitch's hamburgers. Next he removed the bowls of dip that Mitch had whipped up earlier before placing them next to the platter. The chips were already in bowls. Afterward, he set the food on the island and reached back inside the fridge to grab four beer bottles. He noticed the night before that Bobby had ordered a beer, so he was guessing the brew would be okay with him. But if the younger man didn't want any, he'd come back in and grab him water or a soda.

He pulled the tray from under the cabinet, then he set the dips, chips and beers on it.

"I'll help," Mitch said as he strolled into the kitchen.

Jace handed him the plate of meat. "How did it go with Cody?"

"He just got in from a three-day field exercise. He's headed to bed but said he'd be up for a visit in the morning. I figured we could leave after breakfast and drive up."

"Sounds good. Let's see if Bobby wants to join us."

Mitch nodded before he turned and led the way back outside. Piper and Bobby were sitting side by side in matching wooden lounge chairs. They had their heads together and were speaking quietly.

Piper looked up and met his gaze, and he was glad to see the distress from earlier was seemingly gone. She smiled, so he detoured to walk by her and placed a small kiss against her lips.

"Beer?" he asked after he'd pulled back.

"Please," she smiled at him. He lowered the tray so she could reach for the bottle.

"Bobby? If you want water or a soda, that's fine too."

"I'll take a beer," Bobby told him.

Jace let him pick his drink before taking the tray over to the table. He unloaded, setting everything across the top before lifting up the remaining drinks.

Mitch was fiddling with the barbeque knobs when Jace joined him.

"Here you go, man," Jace offered, holding out the cold beer.

"Thanks. We'll give it a couple of minutes to heat up."

"Sure," Jace agreed. "I have to thank you for coming up here and helping. I really owe you, man."

"Are you kidding?" Mitch chuckled. "As soon as I woke up, I started researching anything and everything I could on shifter lore. Werewolf and skin walker lore, also."

Since Jace had done the same, he shrugged. "Still I couldn't trust just anyone with this. Piper means too much to me. I want her to accept what she has inside her, so she'll be happy."

"Like I told her, we'll figure this out, but I do think that you'll both have to change some of your thinking."

"How do you mean?"

"You and Piper act like her wolf is separate, but it's a part of her. It's like you talk about the wolf as a 'her' but wouldn't the 'her' still be Piper? And Piper always says 'my wolf felt' instead of 'I felt'."

Having not realized it, Jace thought about Mitch's words and could see his buddy had a point.

"It surprised me when Piper said she called herself a werewolf and not a shifter. I think she's still running from what she is," Mitch commented.

Well damn, Jace knew that, didn't he? Every day Jace had to push Piper to talk about her wolf and ask if she wanted to shift. She'd started to look forward to it but he still brought it up. Maybe he needed to help her more. If Mitch could see she wasn't fully undertaking her gift, what about Bobby?

Maybe they needed to shift even more. He glanced around the yard, taking in one of his favorite spots.

The entire house was surrounded by trees and situated between the private beach and road. Now that he knew Bobby had been able to see into the back, he wondered if he needed to beef up security or not.

Of course Bobby had purposely been spying, but if he was going to have both Piper and Bobby transforming into wolves then better coverage for privacy would be needed.

"What are you thinking about?" Mitch bumped his arm.

"If Bobby was able to see Piper shift yesterday, we probably need to make sure we have better shelter out here."

"Yeah that would be smart. We can build something that will fit the décor and still conceal it a little better."

Jace was just so overwhelmed with Mitch's generosity. He felt stupid and ashamed that he'd been jealous of his best friend earlier. While Mitch came across big and bad at first glance, there was not a better man than Mitch Bryant.

"Thanks, man," Jace said as he faced his buddy. "For all of this."

"Hell," Mitch said, dropping his voice just a little. "It's so obvious that you're totally in love with her. Isn't that why you left the unit? To settle down and hopefully find your soul mate?"

Jace laughed. "It is."

"Besides, you'd do the same for me."

Jace squeezed Mitch's shoulder. "I would – will – if you ever need me."

Mitch nodded. "I know. Plus *shit*, this is just so cool!"

And that was why Mitch was his best friend. "Come on, man. Let's get the food started."

* * * *

Piper hated riding in a car for long periods of time. She'd done so much traveling when she'd been running from Joe, and now that she'd settled down with Jace, she couldn't find anything good about road trips.

Since she was struggling to remain calm, she worried that Bobby was handling the trip even worse than her. But every time she glanced over at him, Bobby was staring out of the window at the passing scenery or talking to Mitch.

She'd offered Mitch the front seat since his legs were longer and he was so much bigger than she was. So for most of the drive Mitch was seated sideways so he could look back and talk to them.

He was currently telling a story about when he and Jace, along with the rest of the team, had gotten food poisoning from a street vendor in some country he refused to name. Jace kept his attention on the road as he drove but by the little smile on his face, he was listening to his friend.

Piper enjoyed Mitch's stories, even if he didn't give them all the details. She could tell when he was holding back. But it made her think about Jace's life before they'd met. Of course she knew that Jace had spent most of his life in the service. His father had also been military and it was a family tradition that Jace had followed. The fact that he'd grown up a military brat—his words—was one of the reasons he was so intent in settling down.

He'd bought the bar soon after he'd retired. But sometimes she wondered if he missed his old life. It would kill her if he regretted leaving behind his first career. She needed him, though. Every day it was more apparent that she was a better person with Jace around.

He supported and loved her. He accepted the animal inside her. She couldn't imagine having to try to manage all the changes in her life without him. Plus, both he and Mitch had been wonderful with Bobby. Just the fact that they were willing to drive all the way to San Diego on the small chance that one of their old teammates had information to help made her grateful for them.

She hoped they were making the right decision sharing what they were with someone else. Jace had said that they wouldn't reveal themselves right away. They'd share a similar story like Cody had witnessed and see how he responded. Piper was good with the plan so far. If Cody reacted positively to their story then they would decide how much he should know.

She still couldn't believe that everything was happening so fast. Just as Mitch had arrived, Bobby had shown up, and now they were headed to yet another stranger's place.

"How well do you know this guy?" Bobby asked Mitch.

"We served in the same unit at the end of Jace's commission. Right after Jace left, I transferred units. I think we had a couple of missions with him?" Mitch asked Jace.

"One, my last. It went textbook perfect and only lasted a week. He seemed like an all right guy but we didn't have time to bond. Not like my other guys," Jace explained.

"I've been with him for three jobs as some of our missions overlapped," Mitch told them. "We'll stay a little cautious, but from everything I've read on him, Cody's trustworthy."

"And just how much hacking do you do?" Bobby questioned, although his tone was edged with amusement.

"Well." Mitch chuckled. "I don't think I'll divulge that. Secrets of the trade and all that."

"I'm surprised you didn't say you'd have to kill us if you told us," Piper teased.

"Actually…" Mitch laughed. "I thought about it."

"How did you learn your computer skills?" Piper questioned. She didn't think that was something he learned in the military as they would have guarded their records better.

"Oh, I've picked up a few things here and there."

Jace snorted. "Mitch is actually a genius. One of the highest IQs in the military.

Piper did a double-take at the big tattooed guy in the front seat.

"Ah, shut up, man!" Mitch whined. He actually whined!

Bobby snickered, and Piper couldn't hold back her own mirth. They slumped toward one another as the laughter erupted from them.

"Hey!" Mitch protested which sent them on a bigger fit.

Wiping the tears out of her eyes, she tried to get a hold of herself. It took several attempts since every time she thought she was through, Bobby would giggle and she'd lose it again.

When she finally was sure she was okay, she leaned up and patted Mitch's shoulder. "I should have known. You're one of those people that are too smart for their own good."

"You got that right," Jace agreed.

"Screw you all! Laughing at me." Mitch crossed his arms over his chest but when he glanced back at them, he winked.

"I think we're close." Jace leaned forward to stare out of the windshield. "What's his street again?"

Mitch pulled out his cell and pushed a few buttons. "He lives on Knight. There's the supermarket he mentioned," Mitch replied pointing. "It should be three streets down and on the right."

Now that they were almost to Cody's house, fear shot through Piper's body. When Bobby's hand covered hers, she looked over and saw the same expression on his face. She needed to keep it together—if not for herself, for Bobby.

She clasped her fingers around his. "It's going to be all right. We'll be safe," she tried to assure him.

Bobby nodded but his eyes kept darting from her to back outside the window.

"Just for now, I think we should proceed with caution but be open to what Cody says," Jace brought up.

She didn't want Jace to worry. For now she'd keep that just between Bobby and herself. Maybe things wouldn't have to change. Hopefully any talk of being an Alpha would go away. "Sounds good to me," she said sincerely.

Mitch and Bobby agreed.

The house that came into view was an older row house that was in need of a new paint job but had beautiful landscaping. The garage door was open, showing a large collection of tools and yard equipment.

It was obvious that whoever owned that equipment had a talent. The grass and bushes, small trees and flower planters were arranged artfully. No wonder he didn't have time to work on the outside of his house. It must have taken forever to accomplish what he had with all the blossoms.

"Wow!" Piper exclaimed. While her and Jace's backyard was full of gorgeous arrangements, it was nothing compared to this house.

"Guess Cody has a green thumb," Mitch added. "That's not in his file."

Piper grinned. She wondered if that meant Mitch planned to find out if anything else had been left out in his secret dossiers.

As they pulled into the driveway, a man stepped out from beside the house. He looked in his late thirties with dark, short hair. He was wearing a ratty pair of jean shorts and a black tank top. Muscles and tattoos wound down his shoulders to his wrists.

Bobby gasped beside her. Piper was pretty sure the next word out of his mouth would be a repeat of her 'wow' from earlier. Instead he bit his bottom lip.

Well, if Bobby was feeling well enough to check out the nice scenery, maybe this trip would be worth it.

Jace waved as their SUV came to a stop. "Here we go," he murmured. They climbed out of the car and headed straight toward Cody.

Cody's smile was welcoming as introductions were made. Bobby and Cody's handshake lasted a little longer than everyone else's but she didn't think Jace or Mitch noticed.

"Your landscaping is amazing," Piper complimented.

"Thank you." Cody waved his hand toward a half complete flower bed. "I was trying to find something to do with my time when I wasn't on a mission or in training. I started just looking at trees and bushes but over time, I've added as much as I can. I like being out in the sun. Plus San Diego is a perfect environment for some of these plants."

"It shows you've worked hard on them," Bobby said quietly.

A look passed between Cody and Bobby. The attraction between the two was clearly a two-way street. She glanced over at Jace and saw him eyeing Cody closely.

"Come around the back," Cody suggested. "I'll show you some of my favorites and I have tea and soda on the deck."

Mitch moved first, drawing Cody into a conversation about old friends. Jace walked behind them. Since Piper and Bobby actually wanted to see the yard, they strolled behind.

"Wait! Do you smell that?" Bobby pulled her to a stop.

"What? Smell what?" The fragrance of the roses and freshly cut grass was nice but not anything to get excited about but maybe Bobby wasn't used to his heightened senses yet. "You'll get used to the enhanced scent."

"No." Bobby shook his head. "Not that. I can smell someone, like with you, someone like us."

"Like us?" she squeaked. "You can pick up the aroma of a werewolf?"

"Well sort of," Bobby said then shrugged. "Can't you?"

"I don't think so." She closed her eyes and breathed deeply. She still could only pick up the vegetation in the yard, the salty air, someone had a grill going and just a faint odor of oil. Nothing else. "No."

"Huh." He frowned. "How did you know about me?"

"When our fingers brushed. I felt the jolt. That's how I've always been able to tell. There is sort of an electric current that I can pick up on. It's only happened with people like us."

"Oh, I didn't know that."

They stared at one another.

"Maybe we need to make a list or something. About what's different for us," she suggested.

"Yeah."

"But right now, can you tell if the other...shifter is close?"

"I don't think so. It's kind of faded but a shifter has been on this property."

Piper glanced in the direction the guys had disappeared in. She wasn't certain if she should be worried or not. But something in her gut told her that they needed to be very careful.

"Okay, I'll try to pull Jace off to the side and tell him. Keep your eyes, or nose, or whatever open. Let me know if you pick up anything else."

"I will," he promised.

She couldn't help taking one quick look around as they started to walk toward the back—still nothing out of the ordinary to her. It was weird, though, that she detected people with the ability to change differently than Bobby did. She wondered how other shifters managed? There didn't seem to be much similarity always.

The night at the bar she had just assumed he had reacted to the touch the same as her. Damn, there was so much that they didn't know.

Hopefully Cody would be able to help. She was tired of being in the dark about her own abilities.

Chapter Seven

Jace was about to head back to the front of the house and find Piper and Bobby when they came through the gate. As they walked closely together, he noticed both of their shoulders were stiff with tension.

Cody was telling Mitch about the house. He'd bought it as a fixer-upper and had completely remodeled the entire inside. Jace could really appreciate the workmanship. The porch and deck they were currently sitting on had also been one of Cody's projects. Maybe Jace would be able to get Cody to help with the additions Jace wanted in his own backyard. He seemed to understand how to merge privacy and beauty.

He didn't want to be rude and leave the conversation when Cody was going into detail about all his work but something was going on with Piper and Bobby and he wanted to know what. Just as he started to rise, though, Piper reached him and ran her hand over his shoulder. He relaxed back in his seat as the two joined them around the table. He hoped it wasn't anything serious. He'd picked up on the attraction between Cody and Bobby. He didn't care if either man was gay. Hell, 'don't ask, don't tell' had been repealed because it in no way kept a soldier from serving his country effectively. But Bobby had a lot on his plate right then and Cody was a career military man. He didn't want to see Bobby heartbroken and left behind when Cody eventually took off.

Piper would surely catch him up later when they had privacy.

"So I know you didn't drive all this way to hear about my remodeling. You said on the phone you wanted to talk about something, in person?" he asked Mitch, but then looked at all the others.

Mitch nodded to Jace.

"We've come across a report that you gave. Something you saw in the jungle?" Jace said.

Cody surprised him with a booming laugh. "Don't tell me you came all this way for that? Hell, man, you could have given me shit on the phone!"

"What do you mean?" Jace asked, confused by Cody's reaction.

"Look, man, I know it's weird. I'm not even sure why I put it in my report. But I've gotten shit from everyone since it was leaked."

That was interesting. Jace hadn't been aware anyone else had seen it. "We're not here to give you a hard time," Jace told him. "We'd actually like to know what you saw."

A dark gaze ran over his face. "Seriously?"

Jace nodded.

"Okay, sorry about that. I've just gotten a lot of ribbing from the other guys. I shouldn't have said anything. At first I chalked it up to my imagination but the more I looked back at it, I just couldn't let it go."

"I understand."

Cody twisted the top off his bottle of water. He took a long pull before sighing. "It's like I said in my report. I was standing guard when I felt someone watching me. You know that sensation. That *itch* between your shoulder blades?"

"Yeah." Jace knew the feeling well.

"So I tried to be discreet and find out who could see me. Every time I turned my head, though, I would just catch this movement out of the corner of my eye. It was weird but I knew I wasn't alone."

Jace had been in the same situation plenty of times. But the jungle did have a way of messing with your head.

"I knew I wasn't imagining it, so I started to walk toward the trees. Since I wasn't certain my eyes weren't playing tricks on me, I didn't call for any backup. I didn't see anything out of the ordinary but I couldn't get over the sense that there was someone out there with me."

Cody's hand flexed on the plastic water bottle, and Jace glanced at Mitch. The man was obviously bothered by what he'd seen. Jace had to believe it was because he had actually seen something crazy.

"Then I finally caught a glimpse. It whirled quickly around and I caught the face of a man. Young, with a pale complexion, and wide, scared eyes. I called out and ran after him, but whoever it was took off and let me tell you, I'm fast but didn't come close to catching him. But the ground was damp and I could see the light footprints, so I followed them."

Cody laughed a little then. "I left my post and, boy, would the captain have given me shit about that if he'd found out, but I know there was someone there."

Someone or something.

"I kept going until I couldn't follow the footprints anymore. That's when I first saw the paw indentions on the dirt. And they were almost as big as my palm. I looked through the bushes and saw a wolf."

Cody stood and started to pace. "The eyes." He nodded. "I knew it was the man I'd seen from the eyes. They were the same."

"Even with the distance from where you saw the man?" Jace asked.

"The eyes were exactly the same," Cody said with conviction.

"Okay," Jace said. "What happened then?"

"The wolf took off. There shouldn't have been that type of animal there in the jungle. But even if one had somehow been there, why wouldn't it attack?"

"And you never saw him again? Man or wolf?" Jace questioned.

Cody pressed his lips into a tight line. Somehow Jace knew the next words out of his mouth would be a lie. He didn't know how he was so sure, but he was.

"Nah, never saw anything like that again."

Jace didn't press. Maybe they needed to share some of their own information to get Cody to trust them further.

"What if we told you that we believe you saw a man turn into a wolf," Jace offered.

Cody raised an eyebrow. "And why would you tell me that?"

Piper laid her hand over Jace's arm. "Because we've seen something similar."

Jace snapped his head to Piper. That wasn't the story that they had agreed on. What did she know that Jace didn't?

"Really? Where?"

Piper shook her head. "We're not the only ones that have come to you and told you that we believe your story."

Jace jerked and stared back at Cody.

Cody's gaze had narrowed. The silence between them was tense. "No," he finally admitted quietly.

Piper turned to Jace. "One of them has been at the house."

"How did you know that?" Cody asked raising an eyebrow.

"We just do," she responded. "Can you tell us about him?"

"I can't. I swore," Cody told her.

Piper nodded. Her eyes met Jace's.

Jace felt dread sink in his stomach. "Can you set up a meet?"

Cody was glancing among the group. "I can try."

* * * *

Piper was nervous and uneasy as she paced the hotel room that they'd just checked into. Mitch and Bobby were sharing an adjoining room to theirs but currently the four of them were together trying to remain calm as they waited for Cody's phone call.

"I have a bad feeling about this," Bobby murmured from his spot at the foot of one of the beds.

"I think Jace and I should meet with this guy before we take either of you," Mitch suggested.

"I don't like that." Piper whirled to face him. "There is no telling what he will do."

"We'll demand that we get together in a public place. After we get a name, Mitch can use his special skills and see what we can find out about him. Only after we're completely sure that he poses no threat to either of you will we even think about introducing you," Jace told her.

"No, you can't go alone. What if they take you or something? I won't take the chance. I'll go!" Piper demanded.

"Absolutely not." Jace stood and gripped her shoulders. "We don't even know who this guy is. We don't want him to know about Piper or Bobby until we find out if he's a friend or not."

"Unless they want to turn you," Piper snapped.

"Baby." Jace wrapped his arms around her waist and tugged her close. "Don't forget that both Mitch and I were members of one of the most elite military teams in the world. We *can* handle ourselves."

Dropping her forehead to his chest, Piper clenched her eyes closed. What would she do if something happened to Jace? She wouldn't be able to live with herself if he was hurt because of her.

"Hey." Jace cupped her face and lifted her chin. "We won't take any unnecessary chances. We'll cover our backs."

She clung to him, needing to feel his hard body against hers. Jace lowered his head and brushed his lips over hers.

"Let's head back to our room and give these two some privacy."

Piper couldn't pull away from Jace, even when she heard Mitch's statement then the door closing. The feel of Jace's hands over her hips was the only thing she cared about.

"Let me love you," Jace whispered against her mouth.

Was there anyone in the world ever able to say no to a request that sweet? "Yes," she murmured back.

Still wrapped together, they slowly made their way toward one of the two beds in the room. Her thigh hit the side and she stopped pulling back slightly. Tugging at Jace's shirt, she helped pull the garment over his head.

They undressed each other leisurely, taking the time to linger over each new patch of skin revealed. By the time they were naked and Jace had pushed her onto the mattress, Piper was ready to beg him to take her.

"I can't let anything happen to you," Jace told her while he skimmed his hands over her. "You're my everything."

She arched as his fingers drifted down her stomach toward her pussy. Spreading her legs and lifting her hips, she encouraged his touch.

"We're a team, you and I," he said quietly. "Partners and lovers."

"Yes," she agreed. Why was he talking? Didn't he know how badly she needed him? "Jace, please!"

He slid his fingers between her folds—teasing, tormenting.

"You have to let me protect you."

"Okay," she vowed. "Whatever you want."

Crying out when he plunged his digits deep inside, she clawed at his back. "More, more!"

Jace's body covered hers as the tip of his cock replaced his slender fingers. She gripped his ass, digging her nails into his flesh.

He thrust in, filling her with one powerful stroke. That was what she needed. Wrapping her legs around him, she held on tightly while he withdrew then pushed back in.

Jace's movements were slow and deep. Piper rubbed his lower back, meeting each drive of his hips.

Like each time they'd made love, she felt the connection between the two of them through their body and mind. Of course, she didn't know what he was thinking but there was a link that seemed to tighten around them.

She reached for that feeling, wondering what would happen. Closing her eyes, she concentrated on the feel of Jace sliding in and out as she held him close.

Behind her eyelids, she could sense something. Piper opened her mind as it was filled with a bright white aura.

"Baby, love, whatever you're doing keep it up," Jace panted out.

Since she wasn't certain she could hold onto the light and speak, she nodded. Jace increased the speed and the whiteness flared brighter.

"Yes!" he shouted, pounding harder.

She clenched hers eyes closed as the glow exploded, raining down to cover them. Jace yelled and she could faintly hear her own scream as they both flew past the edge of climax.

Jace pumped a few more times before dropping his full weight down on her. Her body continued to tingle with little aftershocks, and when she opened her eyes, the overhead lamp seemed brighter.

Tucking her face into Jace's neck, she tried to blink to clear her vision.

"Are you okay?" he asked, petting the side of her neck.

"Eyes hurt," she told him.

"Hang on." Jace carefully pulled his soft cock from her.

She rolled and buried her face into the comforter. The minute Jace turned the switch off for the lights, she felt a little better.

"Thanks," she said.

The bed dipped as Jace joined her once again. "Let me see."

Cautiously she faced him. His fingertips under her eyes were gentle.

"Can you open them?"

Once again she fluttered her lashes before peering up at him. Jace's sharp intake of breath panicked her.

"What? What is it?"

"Your eyes."

What in the hell had she done? Was she going blind?

"Shh, calm down, honey. It's okay. The color changed. It's this amazing swirl of green, yellow and brown. They're not hazel but just circles of the three colors. Here. Sit up slowly."

Jace helped her and wrapped his arm around her waist. "Can you see okay?"

The curtains filtered out most of the sunlight but she could still clearly see around the room. She ran her gaze from the couch to the dresser. Her vision was clear but somewhat sharper. "I can see, but it's different," she told him before zeroing on Jace's face.

She raised her hand. God, he was the most breathtaking man she had ever seen. His dark eyebrows were drawn in a frown, so she smoothed her fingers over his forehead. She didn't want to see him worried.

"Maybe we should take you to the hospital," he suggested.

"No, I really am fine. I just feel different—more aware somehow. But I feel good."

He relaxed slightly. "Do you think it has something to do with your gift?"

"Maybe? I'm not really sure but I don't know what else would cause this. How do you feel?"

Smiling, he grasped her free hand in his. "Wonderful, content and happy."

"What in the hell happened?" she wondered.

"I don't know but I don't think I've ever come so hard in my life."

Piper laughed then laughed again when—for the first time ever—Jace blushed. Wrapping her arms around his neck, she pulled him close. "I love you so very much."

"I love you too."

"But nothing I said or agreed to when you were driving me crazy will stand," she warned.

He sighed.

"We will come up with a plan together. The four of us. And only when we are all in agreement will we proceed. I won't have you in danger any more than you would allow me to be."

"I know. I didn't believe it would work but I had to give it a try. Plus, it was hot teasing you enough to get you to agree to anything."

Piper lunged forward, knocking him onto his back. He rolled, and she ended up beneath him with their legs tangled together. She cupped his balls and squeezed gently. He tensed, freezing.

"It seems I have the ability right now to get you to grant me whatever I want." She rolled her fingers.

Jace pumped his hips and Piper was pleased to see that his erection started to grow. "Mmm."

"I'm already a slave to you."

Oh, she liked the sound of that. "Really?" she asked, before bending her head and licking just the tip of his cock.

She jerked her head away when a pounding sounded on the interior adjoining door.

"Fuck!" Jace swore.

Piper bit her lip to keep from laughing.

Jace climbed off the bed, shaking his head. "Get under the covers," he ordered.

Piper scrambled to yank the comforter down and slid between the sheets. She pulled the blanket up above her shoulders as Jace dragged on his jeans.

Mitch's hand was raised to knock again when Jace threw open the door.

Looking between Jace and her, Mitch smiled and winked. "Sorry to interrupt but Cody just called. They want to meet tonight."

"Damn." Jace ran his hand roughly over his jaw. "Okay, let's decide how to handle this."

Mitch entered the room with Bobby on his heels. Piper tugged the large comforter closer to make sure that she was fully covered. Jace could have at least given her time before he invited their friends inside the room.

A glance in Jace's direction showed a small smirk playing at his mouth. Oh, he thought he was funny. She should show him and get out from under the covers but she wouldn't and he knew that. There would be some payback.

Bobby's face was flushed when he sat on the empty bed.

"You okay?" she asked him.

He bobbed his head up and down.

"Are you sure?" Why wasn't he looking at her?

Mitch chuckled and sat beside Bobby, slapping his arm. "Excuse our young friend here. He heard some loud…sounds a little while ago." He winked at Piper.

That was when she understood. She and Jace had gotten very loud. "Oh my God! She buried her face in the blanket. "Kill me now."

Jace patted her head and she glared up at him. Didn't he just look so damn cocky!

Chapter Eight

Jace glanced around the dim bar getting his bearings. Cody had agreed to meet with there with his friend, although Jace got the distinct impression that Cody didn't actually like the guy that they were meeting. It was just a feeling that he'd gotten when Cody had been talking with him at the house.

That was the main reason Jace didn't want Piper or Bobby anywhere near him yet.

Jace didn't like leaving Piper and Bobby at the hotel alone, but he had to trust that they could indeed take care of themselves.

Mitch stood by his shoulder, and Jace knew that he was also taking a good long look around. "I don't see Cody."

"Let's take a walk around and just double-check the room before we sit," Jace suggested.

"Good idea."

Slowly they did a sweep of the small bar, checking out if anyone seemed interested in them. There were only three tables that had patrons. Two tables consisted of mid-class, office worker type people. The other was occupied by a single older man who ignored everyone in the place.

Jace motioned to the far booth at the back. He took a seat facing the door while Mitch remained standing beside him.

A waitress with an unnatural dyed blonde hair and way too much makeup came out of the back hallway and strolled over to them. "What can I get you guys?"

"Two light beers on tap, please," Jace ordered. They wouldn't drink but at least it would make the woman happy. Jace kept his gaze trained at the entrance, even when the server brought over two large, dripping mugs.

"Keep the change," Mitch told the waitress, paying for the beers.

Mitch pushed Jace's drink closer to him. "You doing okay?"

"Yeah, I just want some answers," Jace told him. "This thing with Piper's eyes? I mean what the hell?"

"That's what I'm talking about. Piper's not the only one I've noticed a change in."

Jerking, Jace split some of his beer. "What?"

"It's just…" Mitch leaned closer. "Don't you feel different?"

Jace opened his mouth to assure his friend that he was the same as always but paused. He did actually feel a little bit off. Sharper somehow. He'd noticed first in the hotel room that his eyesight and sense of smell seemed better.

"Huh," he grunted. "Maybe."

"If this guy can give us some answers then I think we should listen. We don't have to show him all of our cards but we can learn something here."

"You're right." Jace nodded. "Hopefully this guy will be able to help solve some of our uncertainty."

The front door opened and Cody walked in with a man close on his heels. The stranger had black hair cropped short and looked military. Jace tensed. He hadn't considered that this mystery man might have a connection to the armed services. How would a werewolf even begin to blend in with trained military men?

That complication would have to be added into the plan. Mitch hacking into the government files could get him and all of them into a shitload of trouble.

Cody and his friend started to walk over, and Jace openly assessed the new guy. The swagger of the man's hips and easy roll of his shoulders spoke volumes to Jace. This man wasn't just trained. He was a leader. Jace would bet he was an officer. Captain, would be his best guess.

"Jace Anderson, Mitch Bryant," Cody introduced. "Captain Vince Blackwell."

Mitch and Vince shook, then Jace rose and offered his hand. Vince took a tight hold of Jace's hand and he…sniffed him. Actually sniffed him.

Lifting an eyebrow, he smirked at the stranger. "Yes?"

Vince's expression showed surprised. "I apologize, that was rude of me. Instead let me offer you congratulations."

Glancing back at his friend, Jace wondered what the man was talking about. Mitch only shook his head.

"Thanks?" Jace asked.

Vince frowned. "Maybe we should sit?"

Jace slid back in the booth with Mitch following beside him. Vince settled across from him before Cody motioned to the waitress for two more beers.

They waited until she had dropped off the order and Cody had paid before speaking.

"I meant no disrespect earlier. I believed that you were aware of the permanent step you took with your mate," Victor said quietly.

Jace shared a look with Mitch. "Can you elaborate?"

Victor leaned forward. "I'm sorry. I don't understand."

There seems to be a lot of that. "That's makes two of us. What do you mean…the permanent step?"

"You mated with your lycanthrope. I can sense the bond," Victor confided.

"Lycanthrope?" Jace asked.

Victor smiled. "Werewolf. Shape-shifter."

Well at least the guy was sort of on the same page as them. "And you can sense that I was *with* a werewolf?"

"It's a little more than that. You've committed yourselves to one another," Vince told him. "Did your partner not explain things to you?"

The conversation was going too far, too fast. "Let's slow down," Jace requested. "We've come to get answers."

"Cody explained that you wished to speak with me. I just was so excited to observe the mate bond. I've never met a mated pair. And you're still completely human."

That was good to know. He had no idea how he and Piper had…mated? He wished Piper was there with him now, but he needed more answers first. "We appreciate you meeting with us. You don't mind answering some questions?"

"I don't. Cody told me about the two of you. I also may have dug into your files—legally, of course. But I would also like to ask a few questions of my own."

"That's fair," Jace agreed.

"Great." Vince sat back and picked up his brew. "Please go ahead."

"So are you one of them?" Was it right to ask? He wasn't sure but that seemed like a very important start.

"I am." Vince waved his hand. "Don't worry. I expected the question. When Cody called and told me about your conversation, I figured you knew more than you told him."

"You're also military?" Jace questioned.

"Yes, I'm the psychiatrist Cody spoke with when he returned from his mission. The one he confessed to what he'd seen."

"How long?"

Vince shook his head with his brow furrowed.

"How long have you been...changed?"

"Oh, I was thirty. Almost fifteen years ago now. I had a friend who had been granted the gift and he revealed his secret. I asked him to change me too."

Knowing the man had *asked* for the same thing that had happened to Piper and Bobby made Jace's stomach roll, but he was also intrigued.

"What about you?" Jace directed his inquiry to Cody.

"No, I have no interest in being turned. He's shared a lot about what he is so I can understand what I saw."

"So you know a lot about the shifting?" Jace asked Vince.

"Sure. I made certain I had all the information before I asked to be changed."

Excitement replaced Jace's anxiety. Hopefully he would finally be able to get Piper the information she needed. He had so many questions that he wasn't sure where to start. Plus Piper would have more. "Would you be willing to meet with my partner?"

"I would love to. There are so few of us that having another someone to talk with would be great. My buddy was transferred and I haven't seen him in years."

Jace hadn't been prepared for the easy acceptance from Vince. Other shifters had avoided both Piper and Bobby. He looked over toward Mitch. A slight shake of his head told Jace that Mitch wasn't sure either.

"I guess the biggest question we have is what can we do to make sure they…she remains safe?"

"Safe from what?" Vince asked.

Shit, this was awkward. Did this guy really have no problem with people finding out what he was? "Is there anything we need to know about hiding her difference?" Jace enquired.

"Ah, is she recently changed then?" Vince asked but didn't give Jace time to answer. "Normally the person who chooses to accept the bite of a lycanthrope is given instruction on how to proceed. The rules, if you will. We can't have everyone finding out about us."

"And if she didn't want the bite? Was changed against her will?"

Vince's sharp intake of breath had Jace tensing.

"That's impossible. No one would dare—"

Jace leaned forward. "I can guarantee you that someone did indeed dare," he interrupted. Not only had Piper been forced into her new form, but so had Bobby. Vince was being very forthcoming, but Jace didn't want to give the man everything just yet. He'd wait until Mitch had checked Vince out before they brought up Bobby. "And we need to know what we need to do to protect her."

"I understand." Vince clasped his hands together in front of him. "I would really like to talk to her. If I can help, I hope you will give me the chance."

Jace leaned back against the booth. What other choice did they have? This was what they wanted, after all. "Okay," he agreed. "I'll talk to her."

Reaching in his pocket, Vince pulled out a card. "I'm off tomorrow but then I'm afraid I will be out in the field to oversee a training exercise—so the sooner, the better."

Jace accepted the card and slid it into his back pocket. "I'll give you a call in the morning."

The group stood. Jace first shook with hands with Vince before turning to Cody. "I appreciate you setting this up."

Cody smiled but it looked strained to Jace. Knowing his nerves were strung tight, Jace dismissed it. He needed to get back to Piper.

"I'm glad things are working out for you," Cody told him before turning on his heels and heading toward the door. Mitch walked with him, speaking softly.

"Mr. Anderson." Vince stepped in front of Jace.

"Call me Jace, please."

"Jace, I would like to say that no matter how it happened, your woman is lucky to have received such a gift. And being mated to her? Well, like I said, I've never met a mated pair and am very excited for you both."

"How do you know that we're mated then? Jace questioned.

"Other than the fact I can smell her on you?" He chuckled. "Let's just say that one of my abilities is being able to recognize the bond between others. I can even do so with humans. Your link with your mate shines through you. You are human but a shifter or werewolf—whatever you want to call it—has claimed you as their own."

"I don't actually understand what being mated is all about," Jace confided.

Patting his arm, Vince nodded. "Let me meet with your mate. I believe I can help both of you."

As he watched Vince walk away, Jace rolled his shoulders, feeling the stress of the encounter start to drain away.

They'd revealed to an outsider about Piper. Now only time would tell if they would finally have the answers they'd been searching for or if Jace would have to take Piper on the run, once again.

* * * *

Piper knew the minute that Jace stepped off the elevator and was making his way to their hotel room. She sprinted to the door and had it open before he'd even reached into his back pocket for the key.

Since Jace and Mitch had left, she'd been experimenting with the new sensations she was picking up. Bobby had been intrigued and happy to help. She'd found that she could tell where Bobby was, no matter where he hid in the adjoining room. There was a link that if she closed her eyes and concentrated, she could follow to Bobby.

As soon as Jace had been on the floor to their room, the connection she had with him had seemed to brighten. She hadn't been able to actually see where he was, but she could almost feel it.

Having no idea why she could now do these things kind of scared her but at the same time, she was excited.

When Jace looked at her, he reached out and pulled her against his body. Piper let herself be embraced. It felt so nice to be back in his arms. He hadn't been gone long but she hadn't liked being separated from him, not knowing if he was safe or in danger.

"You doing okay?" he asked quietly.

"Yeah, sure. Did everything go all right?"

He nodded before relaxing his hold, although he kept an arm around her waist. "The doorway of our hotel room isn't the best place to discuss it."

Laughing, she tugged him forward. While he had a point, it wasn't really her fault. She just enjoyed having Jace touch her.

Mitch followed them inside, grinning and making sure to close and lock the door behind him. "I was wondering if we would have a repeat of earlier."

Blushing, she reached back to smack him. So they'd gotten a little loud. Making love with Jace was always fantastic but had never been quite so intense as before.

Bobby was sitting on the bed that hadn't been disturbed, cross-legged and anxious. "Did it go all right? Did you find out anything?"

Pulling Piper onto the second bed with him, Jace nodded. Mitch sat beside Bobby and the four of them faced one another.

"Cody's friend Vince is like the two of you," Jace informed them. "Although, he asked to be changed and seems to have accepted it, even enjoys 'the gift', as he called it. Plus, he did seem knowledgeable."

"That's good," Piper stated. "Isn't it?"

"I think so. He seemed really surprised that we didn't know much about your transformations. He was shocked when I mentioned you'd been turned against your will."

"What did he say?" she asked.

"Just that it wasn't normal."

"Between Piper and myself—both of us not having a choice—I can't see his reasoning," Bobby spoke up.

"Yeah, he picked up that I was with Piper but we didn't mention you," Jace told him. "He could meet early in the morning. I'd like to get a feel for him before we bring in Bobby."

"Thank you," Bobby said softly.

"I'd like to meet him too," Piper agreed. "Especially before we do introduce him to Bobby. Do you think it's safe?"

Shrugging, Jace turned toward her. "I think so but I don't see what choice we have. If we want his help, you'll have to talk to him."

"I can stay with Bobby while the two of you go," Mitch offered.

"Won't he think that's weird? If you don't show up?" Bobby asked.

"No, I think it'll be fine. This really is a good chance we have, so we need to take advantage but be cautious," Jace assured. "There was one more thing."

Searching Jace's face, Piper couldn't imagine what was coming. Jace had tensed and was looking her in the eye.

"The first thing he said to me was to congratulate me on our mating."

"What?" Piper jumped to her feet. "Mating... We... Jace?"

"It's okay," Jace told her as he rose to his feet. "Don't freak out, Piper."

"Don't freak out?" she yelled. "I did something to you! I'm sorry. I am so, so sorry, I swear I didn't mean to." How could this have happened? She promised herself that she would never hurt Jace and she didn't even know how she'd done it.

"Baby, come here." Jace walked toward her.

"No," she said, backing away. Obviously she couldn't control herself around Jace.

"Guys, can you give us a few minutes?"

"Yeah, sure. Let's see what room service has to offer, Bobby," Mitch said quietly.

Piper didn't even glance in their direction as they went through the adjoining door. She stared at Jace. Was he different? Would he have to go through the pain of shifting like she did? Why in the hell hadn't she been more careful?

"You have to calm down," Jace told her, taking a step forward every time she took one back.

Shaking her head, she tried to put more distance between them. Her back hit the wall, and Jace grinned at her. He closed the distance and braced his hands against the wall on either side of her head. "I'm fine. There is nothing wrong with me."

"Are... Are you sure?"

"My vision is sharper, my hearing better, and I feel great," Jace told her.

"But what about turning?"

"I don't think we have to worry about that. You didn't bite me, and I didn't drink your blood. I think this might be a good thing."

"What if it's not?" Piper asked. She noticed her voice shaking and swallowed. "Jace, we don't know what this could mean for you."

Leaning closer, Jace gently brushed his lips over hers. "It means that we are closer than before. That the bond between us is, in fact, a connection that can't be broken. I love you and I know you feel the same."

Piper ran her palms over Jace's chest, just needing to touch him, to assure herself that he really was unharmed. She would meet with this Vince guy and assure herself that she hadn't endangered Jace.

"Vince even said that I was fully human."

"Really?"

"How about you make sure I'm still me," he suggested, rubbing his lower body against hers.

She felt his erection and shuddered. She shouldn't let him distract her. They needed to be careful until she was sure that whatever she'd done to Jace would have no horrible side effects.

But when Jace's teeth nipped the side of her neck, she felt her resolve shake.

"I have to have you," he whispered.

She tightened her hands against his shirt, rumpling the material.

Jace slid his knee between her legs and pressed her harder into the wall.

Oh, that felt good. His mouth covered hers and she opened, giving him access to take control. Closing her eyes, she gave herself over to his power as she yanked the back of Jace's shirt until he pulled back and tore the garment over his head.

"You too. I want you naked."

They took turns undressing one another, only stopping briefly to exchange hungry kisses. When Jace tried to guide her to the bed, she shook her head. "No, here."

"Fuck, baby," he groaned. "You can't say things like that."

Piper laughed and gripped his shoulder, pulling him against her. "Come on. Make me yours."

Jace grasped her hips and lifted her off her feet. She wrapped her legs around his waist. With her shoulders braced against the wall, she dug her nails into Jace's shoulder. "Now, now," she demanded.

Positioning his cock against her pussy, he started to push inside.

"Yes," she hissed.

Jace's gaze locked on hers as he buried himself deeply. His bright blue eyes were shining with love. She shuddered at the look of devotion and knew they needed this.

Connection, bond or link. It didn't matter what they called what was happening between them.

Piper knew they belonged together.

Chapter Nine

Jace leaned forward to stare out of the windshield at the building that Vince had texted him the address of. Vince had told him that this location was secure and they wouldn't have to worry about anyone interrupting them.

Beside him, Piper rubbed her hands on the legs of her jeans. "It's big," she commented.

The building didn't have a sign but was new construction of concrete and steel. It looked clean and well maintained.

"Are you sure this is the address?" she asked.

Jace glanced at the GPS on his phone. "I think so."

"Okay." Piper nodded before opening her door. "Let's get this over with. I feel like I might throw up."

She was looking a little pale. "Hey." He reached for her hand before she could climb out of the car. "Mitch and Bobby know where we are. Plus you're pretty bad ass when you shift, and I can take care of myself. Everything is going to be okay. We asked Vince to meet somewhere private."

"I know." She squeezed his hand.

They exited the vehicle and met around the front of the car. Piper slid her hand into his, and they strolled up the sidewalk to the glass front door.

Jace darted his gaze around, trying to get a good look of everything. Since there was no sign indicating what the building was, he remained alert. He let Piper enter first but followed close behind. Vince came out of an office and smiled at them.

"That's him," Jace whispered.

Piper stiffened as Vince walked forward

Holding out his hand, he offered Jace a greeting first. "Jace. And you must be his mate."

When Piper placed her hand in Vince's, the man's eyes widened. "Wow!"

Piper looked over at Jace.

"I'm sorry." Vince patted Piper's hand, which he still had possession of. "I wasn't expecting such a strong lycanthrope."

Piper only nodded.

"I am so pleased to meet you. I'm Vince Blackwell."

"Piper. And thanks for meeting with us."

"Of course. I have to admit that I was very eager to meet you. The fact that you and Jace have mated... That is so remarkable. I hope one day to meet someone I care so deeply about."

"Yes, we would like to talk to you about the mate thing. Among other...subjects," Piper stated.

"Yes. Well, please, let's go inside. I'm borrowing this office from a friend but he's promised that we won't be disturbed."

"What is this place?" Jace asked.

"Oh, some of my buddies are starting up their own business. They haven't actually moved in yet, so the place was available."

That didn't really answer Jace's question but he let it slide for now. The office that Vince led them to was sparse. A lone, small metal desk with a chair behind it and two matching chairs against the wall were the only objects in the room.

"Sorry about the lack of furniture but like I said, they haven't actually moved in yet."

"Sure." Jace kept his hand on the small of Piper's back until she sat. He took his seat next to her.

Instead of going around the desk, Vince hopped up on the edge of it.

Vince's position made Jace feel more comfortable, like they weren't there for an interview or something. He wondered if Vince knew—and figured he did.

"Jace told me very little about you. If you don't mind, I'd really like to hear about how you were changed," Vince said to Piper.

She glanced over at Jace, and he nodded.

While Piper told her story, Jace watched Vince closely. He'd heard Piper's words several times but it never got easier. He hated the fact that she had gone through so much. If Joe wasn't already dead, Jace would be out hunting him down.

After Piper had explained about her escaping and going on the run, Vince was rubbing his chin. "Did you ever see this man again?"

Shifting in her chair, Piper nodded. "He finally caught up with me. He attacked and I didn't have a choice. I killed him."

Vince's eyebrows rose in apparent shock. "You killed the lycanthrope that made you?"

"She had to," Jace defended.

"No, of course." Vince raised his hands. "I guess that came out wrong. It's just that from everything I've ever heard, the bond between the one who turns a lycanthrope is unbreakable. I've never heard of anyone beating their maker. It's amazing."

Jace wasn't certain how to take that comment. Piper was devastated she'd had to kill Joe.

"I..." Piper clenched her hands. "I wouldn't have if he would have left me alone."

"It would have been easy enough to track you. With the sharing of blood, he would have eventually found you."

Piper's head snapped back to Jace. He knew she was thinking the same thing he was. Did that mean that the two men who'd turned Bobby would find him?

"What happened to him? This man?"

Piper ducked her head.

"He won't be found," Jace said firmly. He'd made sure that no one would ever find the body.

"You were there?" Vince questioned.

"Yes."

"That makes more sense. The only connection stronger would be that of a mate."

"We...uh, weren't mated at the time," Piper spoke up.

"Call me a romantic but I think once the two of you met, you started down the road to bonding."

"Like fate?" Piper asked.

"Exactly, and now that you don't have your maker to train you, I'd be happy to step in. How often do you shift?"

"A couple times a week," Piper responded and scooted forward on her chair. Piper was a lot more comfortable with this subject and it showed.

"That's good." Vince sounded pleased. "The more you let your wolf loose, the stronger the relationship will become. The one thing you don't want to do is fight the transformation."

Since Piper had spent several years doing just that, they knew already for her to accept the change as it came. As soon as she'd opened herself up to the wolf, she'd become calmer and more in control.

"How do you recognize our kind?" Vince asked next.

"What do you mean?"

"It seems that there are different ways that one lycanthrope senses another. My friend got a flash of their animal in the eyes and I can smell them. I've heard several different stories."

"Jolt. I get a little electric static when I touch them."

"That's a new one. Fantastic!"

Vince's enthusiasm was almost catching. Piper grinned. "I guess, now that I know what it is. The first couple times were literally shocking."

"I bet," Vince said with a laugh.

"Is there…? Does it always hurt so much to shift?"

Vince's amusement faded. "It does. When I was first learning, my mentor would make sure I had pain reliever for before and after. I've gotten faster but yes, it still hurts."

Piper's shoulder slumped, so Jace covered her hand with his and held her fingers.

"Can you tell us any more about the mating?" Jace asked.

"Well, I can only share with you what I've heard. Like I said before, I'd never met a mated pair. I didn't even know it was possible to mate with someone purely human."

"So Jace *is* still human?"

"Yes, yes. Unless you go through the transformation, Jace will remain human, although due to the mating, you will always be connected. You'll be able to find him anywhere."

When Piper turned to him, unshed tears pooled in her eyes. If they had been alone, Jace would have taken her in his arms. She'd been so worried about that, scared to death that she had taken from him what had been taken from her — the choice

"Although I would love to see if already being mated made the transition easier."

"No." Piper shook her head. "I won't change him."

Vince sighed. "I guess I can understand that since your change wasn't what most of us go through. But you have to remember that I did choose this. It's a gift."

Piper didn't look convinced. Jace would have to have a private conversation with her on the subject later. He wasn't against being turned. He just wanted to make sure they knew what they were getting into in.

"The most interesting piece of all of this is who made you," Vince addressed Piper again. "Because I have to tell you, killing your maker is nearly impossible. Your connection to Jace must be stronger than anything I've ever come across. It makes me wonder what else is possible."

There was an odd change in Vince's demeanor that put Piper's back up. Inside, her wolf was actually making her skin feel tight. She glanced over at Jace to see if he was picking up the same weird vibe that she was.

"I'm not sure what you mean," Piper stated carefully.

"I've been turned for a long time. While I have heard about destined mates, I really was starting to think it was all a myth. You've proved to be bonded so strongly that you'll even kill for Jace."

"I…uh…" What could she say to that?

"The things that I can learn from the two of you…" Vince sounded almost giddy.

Piper grasped Jace's hand tighter. "I think it's time for us to go."

"Go?" Vince repeated. "We've only just begun."

"No, really," she insisted. Every instinct in her was screaming to run away. To put herself in front of Jace and protect him.

"You're not leaving," Vince told her. Any amusement and kindness had drained away, and Piper was shocked to see the evilness in his gaze.

"What's that?" Jace asked.

Vince waved his hand, and Piper looked toward the door. Two large men stood in the opening. One of them reminded her of a linebacker she'd seen when watching football with Jace. Wide, heavy and a huge solid mass of weight. The short, stockier guy had a crooked nose and ugly face. A boxer came to mind when she spotted him. Jace jumped to his feet and blocked her before she could do the same for him.

"What the *fuck* is going on here?" Jace demanded.

"Now calm down. These two men are my associates and won't hurt you, as long as you cooperate," Vince said, still with that calm tone to his voice.

"Cooperate?" Jace repeated.

"Yes, I wasn't lying when I said the two of you intrigue me. A mated pair, especially with one of the partners being human? That is too important to let the two of you go your own way. We need to find out more."

Piper couldn't believe this was happening. She gripped the back of Jace's shirt. "I thought you wanted to help us!"

"I do, but can't you see how much we can learn from the two of you? This is bigger than just a couple of people."

"This isn't going to work. I have friends who know where we are," Jace said as he gripped Piper's wrist.

"That buddy that was with you last night? Don't worry, he'll be joining us soon."

"No!" Piper cried. If they got Mitch then this sicko would get his hands on Bobby too.

"It won't be bad. We just want to study some blood."

"Look at your own blood," Jace demanded. "But you won't touch her."

Vince shook his head. Jace had moved just enough that Piper could see his face.

"I'm actually very fond of the two of you. Please don't force my hand. Just give us a few samples and you can be on your way."

Like they were really going to believe him. "Forget it," Piper snapped.

"Fine, have it your way, but remember, I tried to be nice about this. I invited you here and answered your questions."

Jace pulled on her wrist and brought her forward. Piper braced her feet as the two men entered the small office.

If she shifted, she would be vulnerable while in transformation. Plus, Vince would be able to change also. "What do we do?" she whispered to Jace.

"We fight. God, Piper, I'm so sorry."

"Not your fault," she assured him.

"We'll get out of this," he promised.

He was right. They had to get away.

One of the large goons reached for Jace.

"Now!" he shouted and kicked out. "Run!"

She darted to the side as the big man went down on one knee, thanks to the foot in the balls Jace had landed. The boxer grabbed at her, but Piper was small enough to avoid him. Jace rushed forward, trying to tackle Piper's attacker.

Just before she reached the doorway, Vince's arm caught her in the chest. She stumbled back as he pulled out a gun. Piper froze.

"I'm sorry it came to this," he said.

"No!" Piper lunged, but Vince was able to pull the trigger. She whirled around and found that Jace had taken a dart in his leg.

"Run!" Jace yelled again. She tried to turn but felt the sharp prick at the back of her neck.

"Jace," she called out as her vision swam.

"Fuck!" Jace roared but she was already starting to lose control of her body. Her legs felt like jelly and she sank down. A strong arm wrapped around her waist.

Blinking to try to clear her eyesight, she could barely make out Jace being held between the two large men. That meant it was Vince who held her. She turned her head. "Why?"

"I've already told you, and I hate repeating myself. Besides, I promise this will all work out. You'll see things my way soon."

She was going to kill him if it was the last thing she did. God, she hoped Bobby and Mitch got away. Hopefully when she and Jace didn't return, Mitch would get Bobby as far away from this threat as possible.

"Just stay calm," Vince instructed. "I'll take care of you."

Starting to tremble while her stomach was rolling, Piper gasped. "No." She had to fight to stay awake. She couldn't give in. Shit, she needed to throw up.

* * * *

Jace's mouth felt like he'd drunk an entire bottle of whiskey, which was weird since he couldn't remember drinking any alcohol the night before. But his head was pounding and his entire body ached like only a night out on the town could make him feel.

God, what in the hell happened? He tried to roll over, only to find that he couldn't move.

He opened his eyes and hissed. The bright overhead lights burned.

"Ah, you're awake."

Turning his head, he saw Vince Blackwell.

The bands across his chest, stomach and thighs tightened as he jerked his body, trying to loosen their hold. His wrists and ankles were also tied down. *So very not good.*

"I will kill you if you've hurt Piper," he warned with a growl.

"Your mate is just fine," Vince told him and motioned to beside Jace. "Take a look for yourself."

Jace moved his head slowly to look. Piper was laid out in much the same way as he, on a metal table next to him. Fury rushed through him and Jace once again tried to get loose.

"Now calm down." Vince grabbed his chin. "I haven't hurt her. I told you both that I just wanted to run some tests. I already took your blood. The rest can remain just as painless. It's really up to you."

Gritting his teeth, Jace glared at him but didn't respond.

"I'm really not a bad guy."

"Fine," Jace mocked. "Then let us go."

Vince gave a heavy sigh before removing his hand. "Come on. You would do the same in my position."

"If you're really already changed then why exactly are you doing this? What do you gain by holding us prisoner? Why do you need us?"

"Everything I told you was true. Except for what happened to the man who made me. After I became a shape-shifter, I wanted to make more. He got upset and forbid me from turning anyone else. He wouldn't even explain the entire ritual. So I made him disappear."

"You killed him," Jace clarified.

"I couldn't. What your mate managed was something I couldn't. I had to have help."

Jace really wasn't liking this.

"That's why I'm so interested in Piper. How did she accomplish such a feat?"

"She…"

"She did it to protect you. Her mate. I have to find out more."

"Now you plan to torture us?"

"Such strong words." Vince lifted his nose in the air as if insulted. "Once my maker was out of the way, I found others like me. We've dedicated ourselves to research. I would like for you and Piper to join us."

"Not going to happen," Jace growled.

"It already has—with or without your consent. I think you both will come around, though. Things can get much worse."

Jace grunted. Out of all the people they could have encountered, it was just their luck that they'd met a crazy werewolf.

"You plan to experiment on your kind?"

"Research," Vince said with a smile. "Only an evil bastard would experiment on people."

Jace wasn't amused. "Call it what you want. It won't change a thing. And I'm human, so what are you going to learn from me?"

"I really am interested in seeing how the bond between you and your mate works. That's all. Can she feel your pain? What will she do to insure your safety?"

"She'll never agree to joining you," Jace said with conviction.

"Maybe, maybe not. You're a trained soldier. Just how much do you think it will take to get you to bend to my will? It might be tough but you're human, after all."

Sucking in a sharp breath made his head spin. "I thought you weren't going to hurt us?"

"All you have to do is cooperate."

Beside him, Piper groaned.

"And there is your mate waking up. We can finally get started."

Jace struggled to lift his head and look back over at Piper.

She was thrashing on the table against her restraints, making a panicked sound.

"Untie her!" Jace ordered. He knew Piper wouldn't be able to handle being held down, not after what had happened with Joe.

"Jace!" Piper cried, and he fought once again to get free.

"Stop! Both of you!" Vince yelled.

Piper's breath was coming out too fast as her terror built. She began to scream, and Jace felt his tears start to fall. He couldn't help her. He had let her down and now they would both pay.

Crying his name, Piper thrashed.

"Shit!" Vince ran to the door and pounded on it. "Get Dr. Grace in here now."

Jace didn't care who this doctor was. When he got free, he was going to slaughter everyone in the building. Fuck, he hoped Mitch and Bobby had got away. They were the only ones who would be able to help. Mitch would be able to think of a way to break in and get both him and Piper free.

If Vince got his hands on Bobby, there was no telling what he would do. Two shifters under his control would be even worse. Bobby wouldn't be able to handle the situation any better than Piper.

The door slammed open and a woman in her early forties rushed in. "What's going on?"

"Give her something to calm her down."

"She's going to go into shock," the doctor informed him. The woman dressed in a white lab coat with her dark hair pulled back approached Piper and drew out a syringe.

"Don't you fucking touch her!" Jace yelled.

She didn't even look at him. Just clamped one hand down on Piper's arm and started to insert the needle under Piper's skin.

Jace bellowed.

The woman finished injecting Piper and turned to him. "Him too?"

"Yeah. We'll have to wait until the woman is stable enough or my results will be skewed."

Piper whimpered.

"Lady, if you come any closer, I swear to God I will take you down," Jace threatened.

"I'm impressed with your selection." The woman spoke to Vince. "And a mated pair... How fabulous."

"Yes, I believe we'll learn a lot."

Even though he knew he couldn't stop her Jace tried to jerk his arm away from the woman's hand.

"Hush now. This will just put you to sleep. Nothing that will harm you."

He really, *really* wished they would stop saying that. Jace bared his teeth at her.

Shaking her head, she injected his arm. "Sleep now."

As hard as he tried to fight the lull of sleep, Jace found his eyelids growing heavy. He could hear speaking around him but couldn't make out the words.

He floated, unable to concentrate.

Powerless to stop what was happening.

Chapter Ten

Piper rubbed her face against her pillow, not wanting to wake up. She felt dehydrated and sick. Jace was breathing hard next to her and she cuddled into his warmth.

The bedroom was colder than they normally kept it. As she reached down for the comforter, her hand brushed over a rough blanket instead. She raised her feet while squinting down the bed.

They weren't in their bedroom. In fact, they weren't in their house. Piper sat up quickly and her stomach rolled when she realized that they'd been kidnapped. She gagged and put her hand over her mouth.

"Piper?" Jace said sleepily.

"Jace." She shook him hard. "Jace wake up!"

"What?" he asked as he opened his eyes. "Where are we?"

"I don't know."

He sat up a lot slower than she had but still looked just a sick. "You okay, baby?" he asked.

Piper pressed up close to him, relieved when he wrapped her in his arms, making her feel safer. She didn't know how she would have survived if she'd been all alone. "I think so."

"I wonder why he moved us?" Jace whispered.

Looking around the room, she was far from impressed by the stark walls. They were lying on a mattress that had been placed on the floor. And there was no other furniture in the room. Both the walls and carpet were a light gray.

"Let me see you." Jace turned her and started to run his hands over her. "Are you hurt anywhere?"

Her body ached and her head throbbed but overall she was uninjured. She'd been through worse. "I'm okay."

"Thank God." Jace embraced her, cupping the back of her head. She lifted her face to brush her lips over his.

Resting her cheek on his chest, she listened to him breathe. Just being in his presence helped her contain some of her fear. Jace was home to her and wherever he was, she knew that he'd always watch over her.

She shivered and pressed harder into him when the door opened. Vince stepped into the room with his two goons right behind him, holding the tranq guns on them.

"I trust you both are well?" Vince asked smiling at them.

She felt Jace tense against her and clamped her hand over his. "Now what are you going to do to us?" she asked.

"Nothing. Dr. Grace has finished running your blood work. You'll be happy to know that it came back completely normal."

"Both of ours?" Piper would have expected hers to be different. That was why she had avoided going to the doctor.

"Well, as normal as can be expected. Nothing *we* didn't expect. Jace is still one hundred percent human. His DNA hasn't changed. And, Piper, while your DNA has marks of a wolf, we expected that."

"Oh," Piper sighed.

"So you're letting us go?" Jace spoke up.

"Not yet," Vince replied. "We still have some questions we would like answered. Plus, more data for my research—the mate bond and all that."

"And how do you plan to test that?" Jace asked sharply.

"Oh, nothing for you to worry about," Vince assured. "Right now, anyway. I want the bond between the two of you in full control when we get started."

Piper didn't think that sounded like a good idea at all. "Just release us," she pleaded.

"I can't. Now, I brought you some food."

Piper glanced over her shoulder at Jace. She didn't want to eat anything they brought her. What if it was drugged and poisoned them?

Vince set two bags down beside the door and started to back out. "And just so you know, we found your friend. He was at the hotel waiting on you two to come back. We have him in another room. If you cooperate instead of fighting, we'll make sure that he remains unharmed."

Piper whirled around to Jace.

"Enjoy your dinner," Vince said then the door closed.

"What about—?"

Jace's mouth slammed down on hers. Surprised, she jerked back, but he caught her face in his hands and kissed her again.

Piper relaxed in his hold. When he pulled back slightly, he whispered right against her lips, "He only mentioned one person. And he said friend, not another shifter. I don't know if they are listening. Don't say any other name."

"Oh." She licked Jace's bottom lip. "Gotcha."

"He's still suspicious about how you killed Joe. He can't find out about our friend. I don't think our friend could handle this."

"You think he got away?" She shook with fear.

"I don't know, but I hope so."

"Okay." She had to agree. Jace probably had a point. There was even more that she was hiding, though. With Bobby in danger, how could she handle it if she really was an Alpha?

Her stomach was tight with worry for him already. She might have been able to keep her secret from Jace and Mitch, but Vince knew more about her kind. Vince might just figure out what she'd been hiding from her mate.

If Vince was this nuts over their bond and he found out she was also possibly an Alpha, she might not survive the night, or day, or whatever.

Glancing over at Jace, she wanted to confess to him. Her heart actually ached, knowing that she hadn't been completely honest with him. But she couldn't take the chance that Vince could overhear. As soon as they got out, though, she'd find a way to bring up her concern about being an Alpha and how Bobby responded to her.

"Let's see what they brought us to eat," Jace said and climbed out of the bed. His jeans and T-shirt were rumpled but damn, he still looked good.

He bent and picked up the two bags before opening one of them. "Huh. Sandwiches and chips. I would have expected that they would feed a werewolf some real meat or something."

Piper snorted. "Are you sure we should eat it?"

"We know they have no problem shooting us up, so I doubt they'll put anything in the food. But no matter what, if we want to escape, we need to keep up our strength."

Jace strolled over to her while she settled her back against the wall. He tossed her one of the bags before rejoining her. Sitting side by side, they opened the sacks and divided the food.

"It doesn't suck," Piper commented, after taking a big bite from the ham and turkey on wheat bread.

Chuckling, Jace nodded. "I had worse in the service."

There were also a couple of bottle of waters and they finished them off quickly. Jace gathered the trash and stuffed them in one of the bags.

"Now what?" Piper asked as she tucked herself under Jace's arm.

"We play along," Jace said softly, turning his head so he was speaking in her ear. "They'll eventually want to take us out of this room again and when they do, we'll make our move. Plus we have Mitch on our side. He won't be just sitting waiting for a rescue."

"I hope everyone is okay," she told him. She was so worried about Bobby. It didn't look like Vince had found out about him but how was that possible? Mitch wouldn't have left Bobby. So if Bobby had gotten away, was Mitch really alive? "We need to make sure they haven't hurt Mitch."

"Yeah, we'll demand to see him."

"Good." She closed her eyes. "And we will get out of here."

"We will and make sure that Vince and his *friends* don't get their hands on anyone else."

* * * *

A sharp pain accompanied him the next time Jace floated to the surface of consciousness. His stomach felt sour while every muscle in his body hurt. Surely one or two didn't though. He'd laugh at his own joke but waking up on the same table as earlier Jace was pissed. "Stop fucking shooting us up."

They hadn't gotten the chance to try to escape the next time the door had opened. Vince had walked in with the same two men and darted them before either Jace or Piper had been able to move. Jace had tried to fight the drug but once again he hadn't been able to.

He'd tightened his grip on Piper. *God damn*, he hated this.

He didn't want to open his eyes and have his head split open. He refused to turn even attempt to turn his head and look around. Soon, very soon, he was going to get out of the restraints and get his revenge. A chill traveled up his spine as he heard footsteps coming closer.

"Mr. Anderson," a woman's voice sounded above him. "Please refrain from using such harsh words."

It was the woman from earlier. He recognized her voice. Cracking his lids open, he glared. "I'll make sure to watch my language if you just fucking release me."

"Sorry. I can't do that," she said, patting his arm. "I'm trying to monitor your vitals, so why don't you just hold still for me."

"Sure, I'll just lie here," he drawled. Did this lady actually think Jace wanted to be here? Tied and restrained. What the hell was wrong with her? He turned his head both ways. "Where's Piper?"

"You're mate is perfectly safe. Vince is sitting with her."

"Why? Where is she?" He struggled, but the bands held him down so it didn't make much of a difference.

"Can you not sense her?" The woman answered his question with one of her own.

"Huh?"

"It was quite easy for your mate to pinpoint exactly where you were. And that was even before she was completely lucid."

"What did you do to her?"

The heavy sigh that sounded was followed by the woman slapping her hand down on the table he was strapped to. "You're not listening to me. Concentrate. Can you tell me where your mate is?"

Even if he could, Jace wouldn't have given the woman the satisfaction in answering. He clamped his lips together.

"Fine. Be that way."

As the woman backed off, Jace breathed deeply. Could he sense Piper? While he knew that he had gained some heightened senses, he didn't think his enhancements to the mating bond worked the same as Pipers.

Piper had shared that she had known he'd stepped out of the elevator when he'd been returning after the first meeting with Vince.

Jace wasn't sure how long he'd been lying there in silence before he heard the door open.

"Anything?" Vince asked.

"This one is stubborn."

"I figured."

Jace peered up at Vince when the man bent over him. He now recognized the man's scent. A mixture of clean sweat, woods and cinnamon. He probably wouldn't have been able to pick up on those aromas before.

"Piper is doing just fine. We've kept her calm but she keeps asking for you. If you'll just help us with this test, we'll get the two of you reunited."

Half of Jace just wanted to give them what they wanted so that he could be with Piper again but he knew giving in to their demands wouldn't help them in the end. He clenched his jaw, refusing to give in.

"Maybe this will change your mind," Vince said as he sat a speaker beside his shoulder. "Why don't you listen to your mate for a little bit then I'll come back?"

Vince walked away, and Jace eyed the small black device. He didn't hear anything right away but when he really focused, he picked up on heavy breathing.

* * * *

Piper was tied to a chair and blindfolded. She had made one mistake. When she'd woken up, she'd asked about Jace. Demanded to know why they'd been separated and what they were doing to him in the next room. Vince had jumped on that detail. Pressed her to tell him how she knew where Jace was.

She hadn't said anything else after that.

The link that connected her and Jace was still there but not as bright as normal. Her wolf was not only fighting against the drugs pumped into her but also at the restraints. It was hard to keep herself centered.

Fear that Vince had gotten angry and was going to do something awful to Jace had her trembling. She couldn't stand not knowing what was going on.

She jumped when the door opened. There was a rustling of clothes but she couldn't tell what was happening. She did her best to remain calm, so she could try to figure out what was happening around her.

Recognizing the sound of Vince's shoes against the floor, she waited. He hadn't been gone long.

She heard a grunt and the sound of a chair squeaking. "Jace?"

"Piper! Are you okay?"

"Mitch, oh thank God!"

"You hurt?" he asked her.

"I'm okay. What's happening?"

"Tweedledum and Tweedledee are tying me to a chair," he revealed.

She snorted. It made her feel better that Mitch could joke. "Are you blindfolded too?"

"Yeah."

Well damn, then he couldn't tell her if there was a route for escape and what their chances were. "Did they hurt you?" she asked.

"No. I'm all right. Just pissed that I got taken. I was more worried about you and Jace."

"Have you seen him?"

"Jace is being a little difficult this morning. I'm hoping that maybe the two of you can convince him to give us more assistance," Vince interrupted.

Piper jumped at his voice being so close to her. She'd been concentrating on Mitch so hard that she hadn't even heard Vince move up to her.

"And how do you expect us to do that?" Mitch questioned.

"I think having his mate and best friend in the same room, not knowing what we'll do to them, will be enough," Vince said smugly. "But just in case it's not..."

Piper cried out when a hand clamped down on the back of her neck painfully.

"Don't touch her!" Mitch yelled.

The pressure eased and Piper bit down on her bottom lip. The surprise more than the pain was what had caused her to make a sound. She would be better next time. She wouldn't give Vince the satisfaction of knowing they were getting to them. They were stronger than that. It didn't matter what anyone did to them. The three of them would get out. "I'm fine," she assured Mitch, hoping Jace could hear also. "He just caught me off guard."

"What game are you playing?" Mitch asked.

"I feel like we just keep going over this. All I want is to finish these tests so we can help any more lycanthropes that we come across," Vince responded.

Piper snorted. "You want to find out how to create more werewolves and use them for your own purposes. You want me and Jace so you can see if you can figure out the mate bond. We're not stupid, so please stop treating us like we are. You have no interest in helping anyone but yourself."

The silence after her rant was a little freaky. Then Mitch started to laugh. Piper sunk back into the chair. Damn, she needed better control.

"Yeah, what she said," Mitch added once he'd quieted down.

"Fine," Vince snapped. "I was only trying to make this pleasant for everyone but I see the three of you won't see things reasonably."

Like this was their fault. Piper growled.

"Go ahead and shift," Vince taunted. "I would love to see it."

There was no way in hell he would ever get her to transform in front of him. She clenched her teeth then yelped when her head was yanked back by her hair.

"There is another thing that I've been wondering about. Can you still have sex with someone else even though you're mated?" Vince asked suggestively.

The bond between her and Jace flared inside her mind. Jace might not be in the same room but he had without a doubt heard what Vince had just said.

"If you even try it, I'll tear out your throat," Piper warned, deadly serious. She had been abused once and would never fall victim to that treatment ever again.

"Then don't push me," Vince cautioned. "Your stay here can get so much worse."

Piper jerked her head to the side and while it hurt, she was relieved when Vince's hand dropped away.

"Now why don't we try something else?" The sound of Vince's voice moved away from her. "How is your connection with your mate's best friend?"

"What?"

"Mitch has proved to be a loyal friend to your mate who has put himself at great risk to help you. I am curious what type of attachment you have to him? Does he being a human keep you from forming a link to him since he's not your mate? If Jace is hurt because Mitch is injured will that affect your relationship?"

"I have no connection to Mitch," Piper argued. That wasn't totally a lie. Until a week ago it had just been her and Jace. But Mitch had quickly become like a brother to her. She couldn't let Vince do anything to harm him.

"There I have to disagree with you. A lycan who has surrounded herself with strong personalities and has gained their devotion, that is impressive. I have to wonder how you've managed that. It has to be your bond with Jace. You're making up your own little Pack, aren't you?"

Was that what she had been doing? No, she wouldn't let Vince put thoughts into her head. He didn't even know about her being an Alpha. He was just guessing. She was still unsure what being an Alpha even meant. She wasn't in control of everything. Hell, she wasn't in control of anything. She relied so much on Jace that she sometimes felt like he would tire of how much she needed him.

"So how does it feel when we do something like this?"

The sound of flesh hitting flesh and Mitch's grunt was loud in the room.

"Stop it!" she demanded.

Piper figured out that it wasn't Vince who was doing the pounding on Mitch. He probably didn't want to get his hands dirty.

"Can you feel each time he is hit?" he asked right next to her, confirming he wasn't the one currently hurting Mitch.

"No, you asshole! I can hear it."

"So no connection to this human? Hmm, that is interesting."

Piper couldn't have said whether she had any link to Mitch or not. She could feel Jace's fury tugging on their link. She could actually feel what he was feeling. She wasn't just getting a sense of him but his rage — even though separate for hers — was right there.

Holy shit! Maybe she would be able to feel Mitch too.

Mitch was breathing hard and every once a while, he would curse or groan. Piper followed his breathing, letting the sounds in the room fade to back. It was actually easier to do than she would have thought.

She tracked each intake of breath Mitch took. She cleared her mind so she only concentrated on him. There was a very thin thread. A connection between Mitch and herself.

What did that mean? How had Vince known?

She lightly touched the link, trying to send warmth and comfort through the strand to Mitch. Not sure what effect she might have on Mitch, she kept trying to send her affection and appreciation to him.

When a hand wrapped around her throat, jerking her out of her mind, she thrashed.

"What are you doing?" Vince demanded. "I can see a change in him."

Piper choked and gagged.

"Get your fucking hands off of her!" Mitch yelled.

"I'm happy to see I'm right about you forming a bond to this human. It's unbelievable. But how are you doing it?"

"I'm not doing anything!" she managed to speak when the pressure around her neck fell away.

Vince laughed cruelly. "Are you trying to convince me or yourself? Don't worry. I won't test your friend's loyalty to you, today, but I wonder if he would die for you? Much like your mate plans to do."

Piper screamed, shouted, cursed and fought her restraints and what was happening. It was uncontrollable. She had barely felt the prick of a needle but she quickly recognized the feeling of drifting.

"Don't hurt them," she begged, although her words sounded slurred, even to her own ears.

"I've gotten more out of you in the past thirty minutes than I have in a day and a half. This is all your fault."

"No!" She didn't know if she had been able to speak out loud but she could hear the word clearly screamed in her mind. The blame and guilt swamped over her.

If she hadn't fallen for Jace, he wouldn't be tied up in the other room. If she had never found her mate, Mitch wouldn't have been brought into their problems. Vince was right. This *was* all her fault. Jace and Mitch had only wanted to help. Instead there was a good chance one—if not all of them—would die.

Tears fell down her cheeks and she couldn't even brush them away. Was this punishment for something she'd done? Did she really keep bringing these bad things to herself or was she cursed? Maybe Joe had known there was something wrong with her and that was why he'd first chosen to change her.

So many questions and accusations swam around her mind that Piper just wanted to kill something. Or someone.

Wait, what the hell was she doing?

She clenched her fists. This drug wasn't as strong as the one they had been giving her. While her mind was a little muddled, if she tried really hard, she could push the fogginess away.

Jace. She knew that was where Vince was headed. She wasn't just going to roll over and let the evil man win. If she was building a Pack, she would show Vince how strong they truly were.

Bobby was still out there too. Since she couldn't ask Mitch about him, she had to just hope that he was safe. Maybe they would get out of this soon and she could take Bobby back home and never let him out of her sight.

After this entire mess, she would make sure no one hurt her family—or Pack—again.

Chapter Eleven

Jace's wrists were raw and they burned from his struggling during Mitch's beating. He had heard every hit. Now he listened to Piper quietly sobbing and Mitch's ragged breathing.

The minute the door opened and Vince stepped through, Jace lunged up, managing to only make the table creak, but if there was any chance of getting free, he would use his last bit of strength to destroy Vince.

"Haven't we had enough drama today?" Vince mocked. He lifted the speaker next to Jace and flipped a button.

Jace could no longer hear Piper and Mitch and he didn't like that at all.

"Your mate is hiding things. I know she did something to your friend. He was practically glowing and I believe the pain faded, at least a little."

"You're giving her a lot of credit," Jace replied.

"She's powerful. I can feel it. This is even better than I could have ever imagined. I had just been hoping to get some good samples so Dr. Grace could compare them to others. But your mate... Wow, she has made everything we worked so hard for worth it."

"You know," Jace drawled out, "if I had a powerful werewolf tied up, I would be worried about her getting loose and getting revenge."

Vince smiled. "But that is what you are for. She won't risk the life of her mate. She might fight, but eventually she will come around. Even if you end up hating her in the end, she would still give her life for yours."

"I wouldn't let her," Jace stated with conviction.

"I guess we'll have to see. But we are going to move on to the next experiment."

Jace tried his best not to flinch when Vince ran his hand over Jace's calf.

"Dr. Grace, if you're ready to join us."

She stepped to Jace's other side. This time instead of a syringe in her hand, she was holding a scalpel. She handed the blade over to Vince, who handled it like he was familiar with the sharp tool.

"I've given your mate a sedative to help keep her calm but she shouldn't fall asleep. Can she fight through the fog in her mind to do whatever she did with Mitch for you?"

Mentally preparing for the pain in no way helped when Vince pushed up Jace's T-shirt and ran the sharp edge of the instrument over his stomach. It didn't hurt right away. Instead the burning started slowly, before moving to agony. Vince made a dozen shallow cuts and Jace had to bite down on his bottom lip to keep from yelling.

Trying to block the connection between him and Piper so he could protect her from knowing what was happening wasn't easy. He wasn't sure how to shut down the link but had to try.

At first he thought he was doing a good job. But when the pain started to overwhelm him, he felt the first small flutter in his mind.

He knew it was Piper. The same overwhelming sense of peace he always felt when he saw Piper started to float into him. Calming and indeed, taking some of the pain away.

He still thrashed and cursed, hoping Vince wasn't aware of what Piper was doing. Shit, how was Piper even connecting with him half-drugged and at least a room away?

Jace's body was covered in sweat and trails of blood by the time Vince pulled away. He closed his eyes in exhaustion.

"That's disappointing," Dr. Grace murmured.

"Maybe I overdosed her?" Vince questioned.

"No, it was a very mild sedative," Dr. Grace told him. "Perhaps she needs to be in the same room."

Vince's heavy sigh above Jace made Jace have to chew on the inside of his cheek to keep from smiling. They had managed to at least keep one secret.

A rough hand grabbing his chin had Jace opening his eyes.

"You will convince your mate to work with us."

Jace shook his head the best he could while he was still being held by Vince.

"It won't just be you who suffers," Vince told him. "How loyal is your friend?"

Jace narrowed his eyes but didn't respond.

"I guess we'll see." With those parting words, Vince released him and walked away.

He wasn't going to give Vince the satisfaction of calling him back. He knew what Vince was trying to do. Jace was a master of playing mind games also. A buddy who had later gone into the intelligence division had often shared some of his training on how to survive torture in case he was ever captured in war. Brian had been killed several years ago or Jace would have contacted him to help with Piper.

However, the tricks Brian had practiced with Jace would allow Jace to get through this experience. He would not let Vince use him against Piper.

He had no doubt that Mitch felt the same way. After Mitch had found out about Piper and her transformation, he'd supported them one hundred percent. That kind of loyalty was rare. They would get through this. They would survive and make sure that Vince never got his hands on another werewolf again.

One chance, just a slip, and they would be able to get away.

He didn't know if they had help coming. Bobby was still out there and there was Cody.

Jace should have trusted his first gut response to Vince. It was obvious that Cody hadn't been great friends with him and hadn't been one hundred percent comfortable.

Although Cody probably didn't know what was happening, there was a chance he would try to contact either Mitch or him, so maybe — just maybe — all they needed to do was hold on.

Thoughts of survival would keep them strong. Resolved, Jace closed his eyes to try to preserve all the energy he had left.

* * * *

Piper waited and waited but Jace was never brought into the room that she was being held in. She'd been moved from the room with Mitch and was alone in the small room with the thin mattress.

Her entire body was sore and she was just bone tired. Piper was pretty sure that the day was one of the worst in her entire life, even more horrible than when she'd been turned and that was saying a lot.

At least she'd had some responsibility in what had happened to her then. If that wasn't a clear reason why never to have a one-night stand, she didn't know what would be. But Jace and Mitch didn't deserve to suffer because of what she was.

She'd always hated what she had become — some kind of monster that she wasn't sure she would always be able to control. Without her realizing it, her view of herself had started to change. Since Jace had accepted her, somewhere along the way she had started to acknowledge that she was still the same person.

Why had she let Jace investigate for her? If she had refused to bring in Mitch, maybe they wouldn't be in this mess.

Hearing Mitch's pain had been unbearable. She'd had no choice but to try to help. Still she didn't know *what* she had done. Vince had figured something out, though. That was why he had gone after Jace.

It was harder connecting with Jace than it normally was. If she didn't know better, she would have said that Jace was trying to block her. But there was no way. He wouldn't know how.

Why couldn't she pinpoint where exactly he was like she'd done at the hotel? She hated not knowing what could be happening to him. If she was going to be cursed with these special gifts couldn't they work right when she needed them the most?

Piper slipped lower onto the bed, hardly able to hold her head up any longer. She clenched her eyes closed, trying to fight the tears that had started to fall but it was no use.

She wept quietly, burying her face in the rough blanket. Her eyelids grew heavy and she let sleep overtake her.

* * * *

It wasn't long before the door opened, causing her to have to fight to reopen her eyes. She turned her head and watched as Vince strolled into the small room and squatted in front of her.

Too tired to even lift her head, she tried to scowl at him instead.

"Oh, Piper." Vince ran his hand through her hair.

Disgusted by his touch, she wanted to jerk away but just couldn't get that message to her brain. Instead she allowed Vince to try to soothe her.

"If you would just stop fighting me, this would be so much easier."

"I'm going to kill you," she croaked.

Vince's chuckle sickened her.

"I have no doubt that you will try. But what if we can come to a better arrangement?"

Piper stiffened.

"You're remarkable. Can Jace really give you everything you need? Can he relate to the feeling of letting the transformation come over you and running free?"

Piper shook her head. "That's not going to work," she warned.

"I just want you to think about it," Vince retorted. "Having a mate who truly understands your gift is something you'll never experience with Jace."

She snorted. Of course she should have seen Vince playing this card. Jace was more than her mate, though. He was everything she had always searched for. Human or werewolf, Jace was hers. "Go to hell," she murmured. "I wouldn't ever be with you."

"I wouldn't be so sure," Vince taunted. "This is just the beginning. No one knows where you are. Help is not coming. And I'm high enough to make up an excuse for Mitch going AWOL. I have all the power here."

"That's all you want," she said with a smirk. "But I will make sure you die begging. There will be no mercy for you."

"Bloodthirsty little thing, aren't you?"

"I guess we'll find out," she answered truthfully. After what Jace and Mitch had already gone through Piper would have no problem taking Vince down.

"We'll make a good match."

"Not even on your best day."

His hand tightened in her hair for just an instant. "You'll have plenty of time alone to consider my offer."

He dropped a bag onto the bed next to her. "Eat."

"Fuck you."

As he pushed away from the bed and turned sharply on his heel, Piper smiled. "Score one for me," she whispered as the door slammed closed behind Vince.

Ignoring the brown paper bag, she closed her eyes once again. If Vince was already trying to convert her over to his side, she had more influence than they'd realized. Hopefully that could be used to her advantage.

First thing was first, though. Jace would want her to eat. Pushing herself up into a sitting position was even tiring. Grabbing the sack, she pulled out her dinner.

* * * *

Jace paced the small room he'd been moved into. He'd woken alone, his wounds throbbing, but it was easy enough to push away his concern and injuries. Worry for Piper and Mitch kept his adrenaline high.

He wasn't surprised when the door swung open and Vince — along with the two other men — stood in the entrance. Vince tossed a brown paper sack to him, which Jace caught easily.

"Eat. You'll need your strength," Vince ordered.

Jace dropped the bag to the bed and faced his opponent. The glower on Vince's face was proof enough that the man's plans weren't working out the way he'd believed they would.

"Where are Piper and Mitch? I want to see them."

Shaking his head, Vince glared at him. "You're not really in the position to make demands. The sooner you accept that, the better it will be for all of you."

"So you've decided to stop acting as if you're doing us a favor and show your true colors? What's wrong? Can't get one werewolf and two humans to follow your directions?" he taunted.

Vince growled and took a step forward. "*You* need to remember that I don't need you humans. I have your mate."

The words sent a wave of panic through Jace, but he pushed it aside. "And you need to think about what Piper would do to you if she wasn't trying to protect Mitch or myself."

Vince's lips tightened just before he grunted and stomped out of the room. Okay, so it hadn't been the smartest thing to bait the crazy werewolf, but Jace felt satisfied with the exchange. Any little advantage they could get would help in the long run.

Dropping to the bed, he opened the brown sack and pulled out a bottle of water, sandwich, apple and chips. It was pretty much the same meal that he'd been given with Piper. Not good sustenance but enough to keep him from starving.

Vince wasn't stupid. No, the man had managed to draw them to him and easily get them into his clutches.

Jace started on his food, knowing that any amount of provisions would help the battle to come. He'd just crumpled the trash in his hand when a loud beep then static filled the room.

Glancing around, he tried to spot the speakers but they were too well hidden. He jerked when he heard the scream.

Jumping to his feet, Jace ran to the door as Mitch's voice came into the room in the form of a scream.

"God damn it!" Jace cried as he pounded on the door.

Mitch yelled again with terror in his voice. Then his best friend screeched loud, only to be drowned out by an ear-splitting growl.

"No!" Jace slammed his fists against the wall again. "No!"

* * * *

Piper drew her knees up to her chest as she listened to Mitch's struggles. She wasn't sure what was happening to Mitch, but it wasn't anything good.

It sounded like he was being devoured, and Piper was barely able to keep the sandwich down that she'd eaten. She tried to calm herself, to find the link she had with Mitch, but it was no use. Not being able to concentrate due to whatever was happening with Mitch messed with her.

Inside, her animal was clawing to be released. To hunt and protect.

Her skin was rippling and she had to grit her teeth to keep from changing.

The need to transform was so strong she actually became lightheaded. Breathing in through her nose and out through her mouth, she blocked out everything around her.

Gasping and shaking, she fought to hold onto her human side. Vince would probably love for her to shift. She wouldn't give him the satisfaction.

Opening her eyes, she found herself on her hands and knees.

Just then a deafening howl filled the room and Mitch went silent.

"No, oh God, please no," she cried.

Losing the fight with her wolf, Piper began to shift. Her vision grayed and narrowed as pain overrode every other thing in her mind. She panted as she slowly came back to herself. Rising to her four legs, she shook her body.

Scents were stronger in her new form and she paced the entire area, trying to pick up on anything that might aid her in escaping.

She could pick up on the people—both human and werewolf—that had been in the room before her. Moving toward the door, she sniffed the barrier but the seal was too good and she couldn't pick up anything from outside her room.

Backing up into the corner closest to the door, she crouched and waited. They would come for her sooner or later. If the speakers were hidden well enough that she couldn't find them, she would bet anything that they had cameras monitoring also.

It wouldn't be long now. And as soon as the door opened, she would pounce. She'd kill whoever was unlucky enough to walk in. They'd taken one of hers and she would make them all pay. Piper would get her revenge then she would get her and Jace out of this horrible place.

She stayed alert, and the instant the door opened, Piper launched herself from the corner. She heard Vince curse before a dart hit her side. Landing hard, she growled but picked herself back up.

It was only as she advanced toward Vince that she saw the two men that were always with him holding Mitch up by his arms.

She snarled.

Grinning at her while holding Mitch's bloody arm close to his chest, Vince shook his head. "I expected the attack but am pleased that you're quicker than I anticipated. Now back up or I'll end Mitch's life right now."

She roared when Vince stepped aside, giving her a view of one of the men holding a knife to Mitch's throat.

"Back off," Vince snarled.

Piper slowly took one step away then another. She could pick up Mitch's shallow breathing, so at least he wasn't dead yet. The two goons walked forward, looking at her warily.

They dropped Mitch onto the small bed before quickly rushing through the door and into the hall.

"Now you have a choice," Vince told her.

Vision swimming from the drug that had been in the dart, she tried to get her body under control to take one more leap at Vince.

"I've started the process, so if you want Mitch to live, you will have to do the rest," Vince told her.

Piper froze. What in the hell was he talking about?

"You have about two hours until Mitch will need to be fed your blood. You bite him and then he drinks your blood. He'll live. If not, he'll die. Whatever will you do?"

Finally what Vince was telling her started to make sense. Starting the process...biting...drinking blood. Holy hell, Mitch was starting his transformation.

He'd been changed.

Body heavy, Piper fell to the ground.

"Sleep well," Vince taunted. "You'll be busy once you wake."

Chapter Twelve

Piper knew she wasn't alone even before she opened her eyes. Placing her hands under her body, she struggled to lift herself. Her gaze fell on the man breathing rapidly on the mattress across the room. It hadn't been a nightmare. Vince had attacked Mitch and started to turn her friend.

Back in her human form, Piper remained on her hands and knees then crawled toward Mitch. The big man's body looked so small and broken lying there.

When she got to his side, she was afraid to touch him in fear of hurting him further.

Even though his eyes were open, she wasn't certain if he knew what was happening. She knew how much pain he would be in and how confused his mind would be from when she had been changed herself.

"Mitch," she said softly while she placed her hand on his cheek gently. "Mitch?"

He blinked.

"Mitch, I need you to tell me what to do."

"Hurts…"

"I know," she told him. "I'm so sorry."

"Make it stop?"

"I can't. I wish I could. I'm... Mitch I don't know what to do!"

"Finish it..." His voice cracked before he groaned.

Piper buried her face in his chest and tears fell. Out of everything she'd imagined, she hadn't considered that Vince would turn Mitch or Jace. What if he was currently doing the same thing to Jace? How would he ever forgive her?

"Please, Piper," Mitch whispered.

"It'll hurt," she told him. "The pain won't stop until you are fully transformed."

"Okay, do it."

She shook her head but more at herself than Mitch's request. She couldn't let him die, even if it meant doing as he asked and Vince wanted. She didn't know if it was wrong or right. Wouldn't it be better if she just let Mitch go? He had no idea what it would be like to live with the animal inside him, always fighting and clawing to get free. "I don't know if I can," she confessed.

"I don't want to die."

Sobbing, she lifted her head and cradled his face in her hands. "Please forgive me."

The scent of his blood had been calling to her wolf. She released Mitch and scooted back until she had enough clearance to change. She let the transformation take over.

When she was furry, she climbed onto the mattress and stood over her friend. Jace's best friend. His eyes were wide as he stared up at her. Then he nodded, arching his neck back.

She huffed. There was no way that she would bite him there. She rubbed her nuzzle over his arm.

"Okay," he said softly.

She bit down on his biceps. He grunted before burying his other hand in the fur of her neck. She tried to make the nip as gentle as possible, although she wasn't certain how much she succeeded. Mitch whimpered, and she removed her teeth. Jumping off the bed back onto the floor, she urged her wolf to let her turn back fully to human.

Naked and sweating, she scrambled back to Mitch. Cupping his head, she helped him raise his mouth.

"Your turn," she told him, placing her wrist to his mouth. "Close your eyes. The change is already inside you. Let your teeth down."

The sharp throbbing pain of him slicing into her flesh caused her to hiss and jerk. She barely managed to keep from pulling away. He needed this.

Hopefully her blood was all he needed. Piper had never turned anyone and her memories were still fuzzy on her own transformation. That was one reason she remained adamant that Jace stay human. What if she messed up the changing?

Mitch still might not survive.

Probably another one of Vince's tests. The man himself had declared he didn't know how to turn someone. For all she knew, she could be doing more harm.

What choice did she have, though? Mitch needed something!

Mitch drank her blood until she started to feel faint. Tugging her wrist free, she lay next to him as his breathing grew slower.

As she closed her eyes while dropping down beside Mitch, she started to pray for the first time in years. *Please let Mitch survive this.* Wrapping her arms around his chest, she held him tight, trying her best to protect him now, unlike how she failed before.

The light connection that she had with Mitch before was flaring brightly behind her closed lids. Everything was different now. Her blood rain through Mitch's veins and his in hers.

They would always be tied together.

If this worked, she would be able to help him through the changes coming. Even if she wished that he'd never have to face what his future was going to be like, she would do her best to care for him.

Mitch and Bobby both needed her. Piper had to be strong for them.

Maybe Vince was correct in assuming she was making her own Pack. If that was what she was doing then she would have to live with it. At least the three of them would have one another to lean on.

Jace would be there too and would surely offer support.

* * * *

Jace didn't know what was going on. Judging by the meals that had been tossed into his room, he suspected three days had passed. The injuries he'd received from Vince's experiment had started to heal since he hadn't been removed from his prison again.

Not since he'd heard Mitch's screams and cries of pain.

He demanded answers every time Vince or one of his henchmen threw him food, but they never answered him. It was driving him crazy not knowing what was happening to Piper or how Mitch was. He didn't even know if his best friend was still alive.

The door sliding drew him from his thoughts, and he pushed himself to his feet. Sure he was weak, but he wouldn't give Mitch the satisfaction of showing Vince anything but strength.

"And how are you holding up?" Vince asked, stepping into Jace's personal space. He held the dart gun and another brown paper sack. Tossing the bag on the bed, Vince sneered at him.

Jace opened his mouth, and Vince waved his hand.

"Yes, yes I know. You want to see Piper. You want to know where Mitch is. Seriously, your demands are getting tiresome."

"Then let me go. I'll be glad to get out of your hair," Jace replied with a grin.

Grunting, Vince shook his head. "I don't get *what* she sees in you."

Jace refused to play any mind game that centered around his and Piper's relationship. He knew how much she loved him. They belonged together. The mate bond proved that.

"Doesn't matter now. Not after what I've witnessed between your woman and best friend."

Jace didn't flinch but it was a near thing. Of course Vince would tell any lie to get Jace to question Piper and Mitch's loyalty. That was a predictable play.

"Don't believe me?" Vince asked with a laugh.

"No."

"Maybe you would like to see for yourself?"

"Sure," Jace agreed. Like he would pass up the chance to leave the room?

Vince motioned him forward with the dart gun. "Try anything and you will be put down. And I might get the mixture wrong and make you OD. I'm really not seeing a point of keeping you around any longer."

Stepping forward, Jace closed the distance between the two of them. Vince stiffened but didn't back away.

"One of these times you'll let your guard down. Gun or not, I will take you out," Jace promised.

A hard shove to his shoulder had him spinning but he remained on his feet. The dart gun was pressed against his back. "Just start walking."

The hall that Jace marched through was narrow. More doors along the hall were closed and he wondered just how close his mate and best friend were. Following two turns, Jace had to admire the fact that Vince had put a good distance between them.

He hadn't felt Piper's presence and now he knew why. There was just too much distance.

Vince's hand dug into his shoulder as he reached a door that matched the one he'd exited earlier. "Go on. Open it."

His hand shook as he turned the knob before pushing the steel barrier hard. His breath caught as he took in the scene in front of him. Piper and Mitch both laid on a small mattress naked and bloody but wrapped around one another.

"Fuck!" he cried and rushed to them.

Piper lifted her head, blinking slowly. "Jace," her voice was hoarse.

"What happened?" He reached for her, but she jerked back.

Vince's laughter had a cruel edge to it. "How about I let the three of you get reacquainted."

The door slammed closed but Jace didn't take his gaze from Piper.

"I'm sorry," she whispered. "I had to do it. It was the only way."

"Do what?" Jace asked, desperately trying to put everything together.

Mitch groaned, and Jace really looked at his buddy for the first time. There were small bites over his arms and chest. Dark blood had dried around the wounds and his lips.

Mitch was pale plus his body was covered with sweat. "Piper…"

His friend's pained words echoed in the room.

"Shh." Piper ran her hands over Mitch's shoulders. "It's okay."

Jace didn't understand what he was seeing. He wanted to help, truly, although he didn't know how.

A shudder racked through Mitch, just as he started to yell.

"Don't fight it," Piper told him, pressing against his chest. "Just relax."

When his buddy's body arched off the bed and Mitch screamed, Jace reached for him. Piper grabbed his wrist and pulled him back.

"Come on." She urged Jace off the bed and into a corner. Placing her body in front of his was weird but Jace couldn't take his gaze off his best friend.

"Is he?" Jace whispered to Piper. "Turning?"

Her hand came back and gripped his. "Yes. Just remain still. I don't think he'll hurt you but he is in enormous pain and confused."

"How did this happen?" Jace asked but he already knew. Piper had saved his best friend.

"I'm sorry," Piper replied softly.

Jace wanted to reassure Piper. He knew it wasn't her fault. He'd heard what Vince had done to Mitch. Of course Piper would blame herself, and he wanted to comfort her but the fact that his best friend was in the middle of turning into a werewolf had him speechless.

Mitch's cry bounced off the walls around them. Jace's stomach knotted and he felt sick. He clenched his hands, willing himself to hang onto his sanity. He wanted to rip Vince apart.

Jace watched as Mitch's body bowed back and the transformation started to change him. The process was slower with his friend than it normally was with Piper. It looked as though Mitch was in agony, but after what seemed like forever, there was a large black wolf on the mattress.

The animal was huge! Jace was shocked and just a little impressed at what a massive form his once human buddy was. As a wolf, Mitch slowly climbed off the bed and onto the floor in front of them.

Since Piper was obviously shielding him, Jace did his best to even out his breathing and appear as non-threatening as possible. When Mitch's gaze met his, he could see the human intelligence shining brightly back at him. He relaxed even further.

A few clumsy steps brought Mitch closer to the two of them, and Jace felt Piper tense against him. A shudder racked her body, and Jace knew that she was calling her own wolf forward.

Piper's shift was quicker than he had ever seen before.

She crouched low to the ground before letting out a low growl in warning. Mitch froze before he dropped down on his belly. Obviously satisfied with his submission, Piper approached him with careful steps until she was in a position to nuzzle against him.

What an amazing sight the two made — the large black wolf remaining still as the smaller, lighter one lavished him with attention.

Mitch panted his long tongue that was rolling out of his mouth, and Jace had to stifle a laugh. He would never have believed he would see this scene play out, but it seemed to him that Mitch wasn't traumatized by this change in his life.

Pushing himself away from the wall, Jace joined the two most important people in his life. Piper lifted her face to watch him, but Mitch's attention was solely on her.

Dropping to his knees, he laid a hand on his best friend's neck before burying his fingers deep into his thick fur and rubbing hard like Piper enjoyed.

Making a pleased sound, Mitch's entire body went lax.

"It'll be okay," he told both of them softly.

A nudge to his shoulder had him bringing his free hand up to Piper's head where he gave her the same treatment as Mitch.

He didn't know how long he sat there petting his two creatures but as he did, a plan started to form in his mind. Vince had made a mistake this time. Putting the three of them together only strengthened their bond. Knowing that Piper and Mitch couldn't be used against him only encouraged him to take action.

Under his hand, Mitch had fallen asleep and Piper was calm and resting easily. The link that had been growing seemed to tug at his heart. He understood that what was happening had to do with the unique situation of a lycanthrope. However, Jace wouldn't have been able to describe the strings that connected him to Piper as any other way than magical.

Since he was a career military man, he would have laughed if anyone had ever told him about the wonders he was now a part of. Werewolves and being turned into animals. It was unbelievable but since he'd seen the fantastic evidence with his own eyes, he just had to believe.

Now he was forever integrated into the shifter world. First with Piper then Bobby and now Mitch.

They all belonged to him. They were his to protect and care for.

He wasn't sure where the feeling originated from but he knew that he was meant to be a part of his life, almost as it had been his destiny.

Jace extracted himself from the two resting wolves as he shook the unusual thoughts off.

He paced the small room, and Jace took in the space they'd been locked inside. He called back on his experience of being in tight places before he searched for a way out for all of them. The only door was the one he'd been brought in by—no handle or lever on the inside. So they would have to wait until Vince or one of the others arrived to open it.

Then they would make their move.

A soft whimpering noise drew his attention back across the room and he turned in time to see Mitch cuddle closer to Piper. There was no jealousy as he observed Piper and Mitch.

Instead he was fiercely proud of them. They'd survived together.

Mitch's life might have been changed forever but with his and Piper's support, Mitch would be okay.

Vince was correct in one regard. Piper did indeed have her very own Pack and Jace was her partner. Bobby and Mitch were now under their protection and had their affection.

Vince wouldn't control them or their destiny. By the time Jace was through with Vince and the rest of the people there, they would regret ever hearing his and Piper's names.

Jace moved back across the room and settled down with the two wolves. He wasn't sure how long Mitch would need to recover but as soon as they were able, they would get free.

Piper was strong and if she had to fight, she would.

He had absolutely no doubt about that. Piper always doubted herself and what she had become. Jace had been working on that for the past several months and it seemed that he'd finally started to get through to her.

This setback wouldn't hold her down for long.

He loved the fact that Piper was one of the toughest women he'd ever met but still needed him. Maybe it wasn't even need. She wanted him. It was her choice to be bonded to Jace.

They'd chosen one another. A perfect match.

There would be no way that anything or anybody would ever be able to defeat the two of them.

Joe had tried and Piper had defended Jace with everything she'd had.

She'd been injured—scared and terrified.

In the end she had protected her mate.

Jace let a small smile show on his face. He assumed that Vince was watching them.

Let Vince be the one afraid now.

Chapter Thirteen

Piper ran her hand over Mitch's forehead, relieved that his fever had finally gone down. He was in the very last stages of his transformation.

She needed to get him away from Vince and secure a good amount of food for him soon. The days after her own change were a vivid memory that she tried to bury but she knew the cravings that would consume Mitch when he fully woke.

All the time that she'd spent fighting her wolf part seemed so stupid now. If Vince had done any good for her, it was making her accept what she was. No longer could she wish things were different. Acceptance came at a steep price, but she was finally one hundred percent there.

For so long she'd been scared that by giving in to the wolf, she would no longer be able to control herself, would lose her humanity or some shit like that.

Waking up sandwiched between Jace and Mitch had her reevaluating, though.

Maybe she was an Alpha or maybe not.

Did it even matter anymore?

All that was important was freeing the three of them and defeating Vince.

Sure that Mitch was resting comfortably, she moved over to Jace. There was dried blood on him that she could smell. It was weird that she was able to pick up on the scent.

She'd been shifting more and more, trying to save Mitch. Maybe that was why she was sensing so much more. Carefully she lifted Jace's T-shirt, grimacing as she caught sight of the small cuts up and down his torso.

"It's fine," Jace whispered.

She glanced at his face and found him smiling up at her. "I'm so sorry."

"I'm not going to let you blame yourself for this," Jace told her, sitting up so their faces were only inches apart. "If anyone is at fault, it's me. I pushed you to find out more about your wolf. It was my people that led us here."

"We'll have to agree to disagree. This wasn't your fault either." She sighed before cupping his cheeks. "We'll get through this."

"We will," he agreed.

As he pressed his lips to hers Piper felt the tenderness and love course through her blood. This was the bond. The perfect connection she had with her mate.

Their mouths parted but Piper couldn't stop touching Jace. She ran her palms down his neck to his shoulders. Just being able to feel him and know he wasn't being hurt cleared her mind.

The next step would be getting them out of there. "How are we going to do this?"

"As soon as Mitch is ready, we go on the offensive. Three against three. The doctor hasn't left the lab, so I doubt she'd come with them all of a sudden. We have a chance."

That didn't sound good. "What if one of us gets hurt?" she questioned. She wasn't sure how helpful Mitch would be. "Hell, we are already hurt."

"We don't have a choice. What will Vince think of next? What will he want to test? We do this now before we can't fight back."

Piper wished she could come up with an argument because Jace's plan was so risky, but she didn't have one. She peered over at Mitch and saw he'd woken and was silently watching them.

She placed her hand over his, she gave his a squeeze. "Okay?"

Nodding, Mitch didn't break eye contact. "I'll be able to pull my weight. We get the chance, we take it."

"I seem to be out-voted. It's a plan," Piper said and glanced back at Jace. "How?"

"I think you both should shift again. See if we can make them think Mitch isn't over his transformation. Then we wait for them to open the door."

It was so simple. Piper wasn't sure whether to be thankful or just really worried. She snorted. "That's it?"

"Sometimes the easiest way is the chance you have to take. If your enemy expects a big elaborate plan then by doing just what they don't expect can save your life," Jace explained.

"Trust him," Mitch whispered. "He got my ass out of some sticky situations before."

Of course. Jace was calling on his military background to get them out. But he'd only gone up against humans. How would Vince being a werewolf be different?

"You defeated Joe," Jace reminded her. "If it comes down between you and Vince, I have no doubt you'll come out ahead."

Piper wished she believed as much as Jace did.

"My Alpha," Jace murmured leaning into her.

Piper shook her head but smiled. "Alpha, my ass."

Mitch and Jace both chuckled along with her. When Jace wrapped his arm around her waist and started to push her to lie back down, she went with it. She settled between the two men.

"Let's get some rest," Jace said. "We'll need it."

Mitch's eyes were already closed.

"I love you," she whispered to her mate.

His arms tightened while he kissed her neck softly. "I love you too."

* * * *

Jace was as ready as he would ever be. Even as he watched Mitch's change come slowly, he felt the tide was turning in their favor. Piper was once again shielding him as Mitch turned. Since he wasn't sure how long it would take Vince to come check on them, they'd decided to try to get him there sooner.

He was sure that there were cameras recording them. Their plan actually depended a great deal in Vince believing that they weren't fully recovered yet.

The big black wolf pushed himself up and eyed him and Piper. While Jace was certain that Mitch wouldn't attack them, they had to act like Mitch wasn't taking the shift well.

"Easy." He held his hand out, palm facing Mitch while Piper moved closer to his friend.

He made sure that his hand was shaking as Piper started her own shift. Once again Piper's change was quick and easy. They would have to figure out what had changed for her.

When she was finished, she crouched over Jace and growled at Mitch. Unlike before when he'd dropped in submission, this time Mitch advanced. It was part of what they'd discussed but Jace had to admit that it was extremely intimating to have a huge wolf stalk toward him.

Ears pinned back, Piper snapped at Mitch.

Mitch paused but he didn't back down. Piper rose to her full height and although Mitch was bigger than she was, the power that radiated from her was awe-inspiring. Jace felt it wrap around him in some sort of protective cocoon.

While Mitch moved to the corner of the room away from her, Jace crawled in the opposite direction.

The positions put Mitch and Jace in the corners across from each other and closest to the door.

Piper paced to the center of the room and was situated right in front of the entrance and between them.

It was perfect.

Pressing his back against the wall, Jace crouched and relaxed back. Now all they had to do was remain in place until the door opened.

Piper settled down but every few moments would look between him and Mitch, as if she was keeping them apart.

Jace's legs were just starting to cramp when he heard the latch on the door. He rolled onto the balls of his feet and glanced at Piper and Mitch in the room. Both wolves were alert and ready.

He nodded for them to go ahead with the plan.

The door swung open, and Piper launched herself.

She moved so fast she was just a blur to Jace, so he knew that she had taken whoever was trying to enter by surprise.

There was a shout and cry of pain. Mitch attacked next, darting toward the door that was now clear.

Jace jumped to his feet and ran forward.

Piper was on top of Vince, who was trying to knock her back. Mitch had one of the other men pinned against the hall wall. Jace rushed to intercept the linebacker goon but didn't get there in time to stop him from kicking Piper away from Vince.

Piper went rolling just as Jace took out the man's knees and Jace and his opponent fell. The dart gun that had been dropped skidded farther up the floor as he and his opponent grappled.

He tried to reach for the gun but the man caught his hand and bashed it against the concrete ground.

Jace grunted in pain but the sound was drowned out by a furious roar.

He glanced up and saw that Vince had changed and was headed right for Piper where she was trying to get to her feet from where she'd crashed into the wall.

Jace punched his rival in the gut and tried to scramble to help her but before he could get free, his leg he was caught. He turned and threw an elbow at his opponent's chin.

The sound of bone crunching echoed around the small area.

Jace kicked and was finally able to put distance between them. He turned and watched in horror as Vince jumped Piper.

"No!" he shouted, but it was too late.

Piper had barely managed to brace for Vince's body to impact hers before she was knocked down again.

"What are you?" Vince roared at Piper.

He had to get to her. To help.

Piper's howl was low, long and dangerous.

"Alpha?" Vince screamed the word in terror.

Jace tried to dive forward but was yanked back when an arm came around his throat. Damn it, he needed to take this asshole out.

He turned and blocked a punch with his forearm. The guy had training — that was for sure. He battled, trading blow for blow, not gaining any ground.

Around him, the sound of fighting was loud and gruesome. Jace managed to wrap his legs around his enemy while pinning his throat to the floor. The man tried to buck him off but Jace finally had the upper hand. He pressed harder, blocking all air from the guy.

While he had no problem killing this idiot if he had to, he wasn't sure he had the strength to do it this way.

His arms were already starting to shake and his body wanted to give up. Even with the threat against his best friend and mate close by, Jace was starting to doubt they'd survive this attempt.

The man under him twisted enough to dislodge Jace's hands. Jace threw himself to the side and rolled with his enemy.

Fight dirty. That was one thing he'd learned early on in his career.

He kneed his foe and when his opponent folded in on himself, Jace grabbed him and started to pound the back of the guy's head hard into the ground.

Sweat poured from him, making his hold slippery, but Jace kept wrestling for his life.

He cried out as he was flipped on his back and slammed hard.

Everything went black.

Literally. He could not see a thing.

The weight above him disappeared, so Jace raised his hands to rub at his eyes.

It took several moments to realize there was nothing wrong with his eyesight and that the lighting in the hallway had failed.

A snarl and loud crash sounded close by.

"Fuck!" he managed. *Now what the hell is wrong?*

It was hard to pinpoint the exact location of anyone.

"Piper!" he called out. Vince had figured out that she was an Alpha. What if he had done something else to her? "Piper!"

He didn't get a response. Or if he did, he couldn't tell by the other sounds around him. He opened his mouth again but before he could make a sound, the area around him started to fill with smoke.

He choked before raising his arm to cover his nose and mouth.

It wasn't a fire.

No, he recognized the smell and taste of the flash grenades he'd used himself.

That was stupid of whoever had released one — they would be rendered every bit as unable to see or breathe as Jace, Piper and Mitch. He really wasn't dealing with the sharpest people here.

He knew enough to drop to his stomach and make himself take even breaths. Mitch would also be aware of what to do, but he didn't think Piper would have ever dealt with the smoke. Staying as flat as possible to the floor, he inched forward to the last spot he'd seen his mate in.

Cursing and coughing filled his ears as he tried to tell one person from another. Where in the hell was Piper?

"Piper!"

His answer was a loud rumble before teeth clamped down on his arm.

He screamed in pain, striking out with his free limb. He connected, but not strong enough to help. An ear-piercing howl echoed right next to him, causing him to jerk just as the wolf that had a hold of him released him.

He felt another wolf leap over him as he fell back. Two bodies collided loudly while he scrambled to get away. He brought his injured arm against his chest.

Certain Piper had rescued him from Vince's attack, he tried to figure out what was happening around him.

The pounding of feet came behind him. There was no way that they could fight more enemies. He was injured and had no idea how Mitch was faring. Piper had to be just as exhausted and, god forbid, hurt.

But they wouldn't give in easily. They had to win.

"Lights! Lights!" the order was shouted.

Blinding brightness flared around him. Jace squinted at the figures that moved closer. *What the…?* Those were American military uniforms, although hoods covered their faces, making them appear even more dangerous. The weapons pointed in their direction was not a sight Jace felt comfortable with.

If he had been set up and sent into this location, there was little chance this was a rescue.

Jace dodged to the side, trying to reach the dart gun that had been forgotten just feet away from him.

"Freeze! Do not move."

Jace followed that order. He peered over his shoulder at man who approached, weapon ready and aimed. He sat up and raised his hands.

Waiting for the stranger to get closer was torture. From the corner of his eye, he could see Piper still in wolf form, panting and bleeding just out of reach. Vince lay on his side not moving and Jace wasn't even certain he was still alive.

Bracing himself, Jace stiffened when the soldier crouched in front of him.

"Anderson?"

Jace blinked and leaned forward. He knew that voice.

"Anderson? Jace, you okay?"

"Bri… Brian?" Holy shit was Jace seeing ghosts now?

The man ripped off his cover, causing Jace to gasp.

"You're dead," he managed. He felt lightheaded and dizzy and had to be seeing things. "Fuck."

He tilted to the side, and Brian's hand caught him before he could fall.

A growl came from Piper's direction.

Brian turned and lifted his gun.

"No!" Jace reached out to stop him.

Brian looked between Jace and Piper. "If that's one of yours, you had better tell her to stand down before my men shoot her."

Jace faced Piper. "It's okay. I know him."

It was obvious that Piper was badly injured, but she still crouched for attack.

"I need you to tell me the good guys from the bad," Brian said quietly.

Searching the small hall, Jace noted six soldiers in all. He motioned to Piper then Mitch. "Her and the big black wolf."

None of the soldiers seemed shocked he was claiming two wolves.

"I don't think the others made it. Check the bodies," Brian ordered.

"What the hell?" Jace questioned his friend. He could still remember when he'd heard about Brian's death. Damn, he had gone to the funeral.

"I'll explain later. But first, let's get you all out of here."

Jace was all for that plan. He staggered to Piper before dropping to his knees. He buried his hands in her fur to check where she was hurt. She shook, and Jace wasn't sure if it was from adrenaline or pain.

"Can you get her to shift?"

Jace jumped, not realizing that Brian had followed him. He glanced over his shoulder and frowned. While the evidence pointed to Brian being fully aware of the shifter element, how was it possible?

"Trust me. I'm here to help," Brian urged.

Since Jace wasn't sure who to trust anymore, he wasn't going to put his eggs into one basket, so to speak. He looked over Brian warily, but they didn't have much of a choice. One way or another they were getting out.

Brian's men were starting to carry the two human bodies and Vince's wolf form away.

Jace spun back to Piper. "Go ahead."

Piper's change was slow, and Jace grimaced at the obviously agony she was in. While she panted on the ground, human once again, he swooped her up in his arms.

"Here." Brian started to remove his uniform jacket, and Jace allowed him to place it over Piper.

"You okay?" Jace asked her, holding on tight.

"Yeah, changing helped. What about Mitch?"

Still carrying her, he walked over to his best friend. Mitch looked even worse than Piper. He set her down next to Mitch, and Piper immediately reached for him.

With a whimper, Mitch crawled into her lap. While she rubbed up Mitch's side, murmuring to him, Jace secured Brian's jacket around her. She helped by sticking her arms through the sleeves but allowed Jace to button her up.

It was the best he could do to try to offer some sort of privacy around so many strangers.

"I need you to transform," she told Mitch quietly.

"He may be too injured to shift," Brian said, as he squatted down and joined them. "My men can carry him out."

Mitch rumbled deeply at Brian's words.

Piper grabbed Mitch's snout. "Then change or we'll carry you."

Mitch's eyes closed right before his body started to tremble.

"He really shouldn't..." Brian started.

Piper glared at Brian before concentrating on Mitch. "You can do it," she encouraged. "Shift!"

Mitch howled but his body contorted and in only a few minutes, he was human.

"Holy shit!" Brian exclaimed. "Mitch?"

Jace backed up, grabbing Brian's arm to keep Brian from getting too close. His connection with Piper was telling him how protective she was feeling about Mitch.

"How did she...?"

Piper turned her head and narrowed her eyes at them.

"You can't command a shift from someone," Brian said with wonder.

She sighed deeply before shrugging. "Sure, whatever."

Chapter Fourteen

Jace was still in shock at all that had transpired as Brian and his team led them out of the building. Mitch was being half carried by two soldiers while Jace kept a firm hand on Piper.

"What about the others?" Jace asked, as they reached the main exit.

"Already taken care of," Brian assured him.

Daylight was streaming in through the glass doors, and Jace had never been so glad to see the sun. Broken glass covered the carpet where entry had been made. Jace ignored the crunch under his bare feet while lifting Piper into his arms to spare her any more pain.

"Jace," she protested but he just shushed her.

"I could have taken her," Brian spoke from behind him.

He just shook his head. Since he still didn't know what was going on, he wasn't trusting anyone right then. Even the two men helping Mitch were under close watch.

Clearing the wrecked window, Jace took a deep breath of fresh air.

"Piper!"

Jace's head jerked up as he heard Bobby's call. Cody had a hold of his arm, trying to keep Bobby from running toward them. Several black SUVs were behind them.

"Bobby went to Cody and told him about Mitch being taken. Cody called me," Brian stated, stepping up beside him.

"So Cody knew you were alive?"

Sighing before he nodded, Brian met his gaze.

"That's interesting. And you knew where to find us?"

"Give me a chance to explain," Brian pleaded.

"Jace, put me down," Piper said, as she squirmed in his hold.

He gently placed her on her feet. As soon as she stood on her own, Bobby broke loose from Cody and raced forward.

"I was so scared!" Bobby yelled as he launched himself at Piper.

"I know." She patted his back, but her gaze went to Jace. "We all were."

"We need to get all of you out of here before more people show up," Brian interrupted.

Jace didn't really want to hang around, but he did want answers. "Where are we going?"

"Back to the base," Brian answered. "We'll get you all cleaned up and fed before we talk."

"We stay together," Jace demanded. "The four of us."

"Fine."

Brian marched off, and Jace couldn't help but watch his old friend go.

"What's going on, Jace?" Piper whispered.

"I don't know, but I'll get to the bottom of it," he promised.

"Who is that man?"

"An old friend. One I thought was dead."

Piper slipped her hand into his while still holding Bobby close with her other arm. "Okay, we need to get some food in Mitch. I'm worried about his transition still."

"Yeah, let's go."

Brian held open a door to one of the vehicles. Jace helped Mitch slide into the passenger seat before climbing in the back with Piper and Bobby. He wasn't surprised when Brian took the driver's seat.

The drive back to the base was made mostly in silence. Every once in a while, Piper would squeeze his hand but other than Bobby asking if they were all right, no one else spoke.

Instead of going into the main entrance, Brian pulled down a dirt road to a guard house that Jace hadn't even known existed. The soldier on duty glanced briefly at Brian's paperwork before looking at each occupant in the vehicle closely.

Jace couldn't imagine what the guard thought. Mitch was naked and bleeding. Jace was shirtless and had his own injuries, while Piper only had on a uniform jacket.

The soldier didn't even blink, though. He nodded and waved to the guard house just before the gate opened allowing them entrance.

As Brian steered around the guard and barrier, Piper shivered. He wrapped his arm around her.

"This place feels weird," she whispered.

Jace glanced at her.

"Yes, this is where the shifters run when they need to transform," Brian spoke up. "An Alpha would be able to pick up on that, even one just coming into her powers."

Jace narrowed his eyes as he met Brian's gaze in the rear-view mirror. Brian shouldn't have been able to hear what Piper had whispered. And his old friend sure seemed to know a hell of a lot about what was going on.

"Jace?" Piper hissed in his ear.

He shook his head. He didn't like it any better than she did.

The wide empty land around them started to change, with a landing strip not far to the right. A few buildings came into view in front of them.

"Stay close and remain together," Jace spoke directly into Piper's ear.

If Brian heard him, he didn't show it.

Brian stopped the vehicle in front of the smallest structure. "This is housing. I had one of my men call ahead and prepare a couple of rooms for you all. They are right next to one another. The doctor has also been paged to look at Mitch."

"No doctors," Mitch rasped.

"But…"

"He said no doctors," Piper snapped.

Jace shuddered at the authority that her tone had held. He wasn't sure what to make of it but Piper did make him proud.

Brian dropped his head. "Okay, we can discuss it later if you want."

Jace grabbed the door handle, opened his side then slid out. He reached for Mitch's door, helping his buddy onto his feet. Piper had followed Bobby from the other side. Through the interior of the door, he could see Brian offer his hand to help her.

Just as her palm connected with his, she gasped and jumped away.

"Piper?" Jace questioned.

Brian dropped his hand.

"It's okay," she told Jace but she didn't touch Brian again as she climbed out of the vehicle.

Jace slammed Mitch's door closed and muscled his friend around the vehicle.

Piper had put several feet between her and Brian while keeping Bobby behind her body, as a shield.

"What's going on?"

"I thought she knew," Brian offered.

"Knew what?" Jace asked.

"He's one of us," Piper said quietly.

It took Jace a minute to understand but when he did, more pieces of the puzzle started to fall into place.

More questions. He was tired of being two steps behind. After he got the others settled, he was going to get some damn answers.

"I'll show you where you can clean up and rest. Then I'll make sure some food is on its way," Brian said, but he wasn't looking at any of them.

His reaction confused Jace. Brian had always been very sure of himself and confident. It was almost as Piper made him nervous.

"Thank you," Piper replied, and Brian seemed to relax some.

Brian nodded and motioned for them to follow. Bobby rushed over to Mitch's side and placed his shoulder where Mitch could lean on him and Jace.

Piper aligned herself directly in front of them. Jace didn't like that she was using herself as a line of defense but he understood. Something had changed when they'd been under Vince's control.

Her protectiveness of Mitch and Bobby had grown stronger. She was acting like the Alpha everyone kept calling her.

They didn't encounter anyone as Brian took them inside to where the elevator was located.

The building resembled the barracks that Jace had lived in for many years. Nothing seemed out of place or different. But he didn't understand the itch between his shoulder blades.

Something was going on.

He turned quickly once they entered the elevator but didn't see anyone in the hallway.

They only went up one floor to the second level.

Four doors down, Brian stopped. "This room is free and the one next to it."

"I'll take Mitch in here and get him cleaned up," Bobby offered.

Piper bit her lip. Jace knew she didn't want to leave the two of them.

"I'll remain outside to make sure no one bothers you and will knock when the food arrives," Brian added.

Jace touched the back of Piper's hand. He would let her make the decision but he needed some time with just the two of them.

"Okay," Piper agreed. "Just holler if you need anything."

Bobby nodded, and Mitch started to shuffle inside. Jace tugged on her hand to get her moving to the next room.

She opened the door and they both looked around. It was a small area. Two twin beds with a nightstand between them, a desk situated in one corner and a long dresser against the wall.

"Take your time. There should be toiletries and some clothes set out for you," Brian said from behind them. "Just stick your head out and let me know if you need anything else."

Piper released Jace's hands and turned to Brian. "Thank you."

Jace smiled when she bumped against him before walking farther inside. He knew how to take a hint. And his mate wanted him to make nice with Brian.

"We appreciate it," Jace told Brian.

The sound of the shower coming on filtered out to him so Jace took his chance. He moved closer to Brian. "I'm trusting you with my family right now. Don't make me regret it," he warned.

"I understand," Brian replied. "I really do. Just give me a chance."

Jace nodded before stepping back. Brian moved away but Jace kept his eyes on him until the door shut between them. He heard Piper moan from the bathroom and grinned.

A hot shower would feel amazing, especially one with his lover.

He stripped off his jeans and underwear before he'd even made it to the bathroom entrance. Piper's body was concealed by the cheap vinyl plastic shower curtain but he could see her shadow.

"Need some help in there?" he asked, pulling back the barrier.

Piper glanced up while pouring soap in her hands. "You think you can fit? Because I may never leave the shower again."

He chuckled. "We'll make it work."

It was tight but they managed to both stand under the water spray. The fact that they had to be pressed up against one another? Well, Jace wasn't going to complain.

Piper started to run her soapy palms down his body, and he *really* wasn't going to bitch about that. He kissed the side of her neck just as she reached his cock. He pumped his hips for her but slipped, his shoulder slamming into the wall.

"Damn it!"

She giggled at his curse. He wrapped his arms around her waist and tried to pull her even closer. Her elbow connected with his stomach, causing him to grunt.

"Fuck, this isn't going to work."

Shaking her head, she smiled. "Let's clean up and move onto a safer surface," she suggested.

"Oh all right," he said, disappointed, but agreed with her.

Taking turns, they cleaned their bodies and hair until the water started to cool a little. As Piper stepped out and grabbed a towel, Jace shut the water off. He watched her run the cotton over her body, taking inventory of the bruises she'd collected. Just a few, but even that small amount was too much.

"Hey," she said getting his attention. "I'm okay. You were hurt more than I was."

Glancing down at his torso, he could see the small cuts from the scalpel. Funny that they didn't even hurt anymore. He wondered how long they had ended up being prisoners.

She wrapped the towel around her hair before reaching for a second towel. "Now come here."

In the entire time that they'd been together and the numerous times they'd showered together, Piper had never dried him off. He quite enjoyed it. By the time she'd finished, his cock was fully standing at attention.

"Now, you come here," he ordered, yanking her against his body.

She hummed happily. Their mouths met and Jace drove his tongue inside. It seemed like forever since he'd connected to her this way. Moving his hands up and down her back, he just couldn't get close enough. He needed her to surround him, to know that he hadn't lost her. Prove that they were both alive and together.

Stepping forward, he forced her to walk backward, just one foot at a time. He just couldn't make himself stop kissing her in order to get them to the bedroom.

Piper dug her nails into Jace as she gripped his shoulders. The bite of pain from it felt glorious. "I need you," she murmured against his lips.

If Jace had had any control at all at that point, it snapped. He dropped to his knees and dragged her down with him, covering her body.

She tilted her head back and he attacked her neck with his lips and teeth. Her unique flavor burst onto his tongue, causing him to groan deeply. Piper went wild under him, bucking her hips up and grabbing at his.

"In me! I need you in me," she pleaded.

Not exactly the seduction he'd planned, but he wasn't able to resist her command.

Scooting down her body, he used his tongue to bring her pleasure. First her nipples then her stomach before he reached her sweet, moist pussy.

Burying his face into her wet folds, he plunged a finger deep inside her.

She wasn't able to remain still. Her legs moved restlessly as her body shuddered and shook. He knew she was close. He wanted her to go over the edge at least once before he took her with his cock.

"Jace," she moaned, her body arching as she climaxed.

He worked his tongue and fingers inside her, making sure she was thoroughly satisfied before lifting his head. Her hair had come out of the towel and was covering half her face as she lay there, struggling to catch her breath. He climbed back up, pushing the wet strands away.

Piper grasped him by the back of his neck, bringing his mouth to hers. Jace ran his tongue over her bottom lip before nipping slightly. Her body jerked and she smiled.

"I'm not nearly done with you," he said softly.

"Better not be," she responded with a wink. When her hand closed over his throbbing erection he grunted. "Because I still want to feel you pounding me."

"Christ!" Jace blew out a breath, trying to get a hold of himself.

Piper just laughed, stroking him faster.

"St…stop," he spoke but since he was thrusting into her palm, there wasn't much conviction behind the order. Any minute he was going to shoot his load.

He broke away and pointed a finger at her. "Naughty," he accused.

She widened her eyes in innocence. Even desperate and full of need, every moment of making love with Piper was perfect. He'd never had another lover that could tease him to the point of breaking.

He lifted his eyebrow in challenge.

Something between a laugh and shout escaped as he positioned her on her hands and knees.

"Oh yes," she practically purred when he knelt up behind her.

Jace rubbed two digits against her clit while with his free hand he grasped his cock. He placed just the head at her entrance, he paused. "You ready for me, baby?"

"Please!"

With his hands on her hips, he slowly, *very slowly* started to breach her.

He knew his woman well. She tried to push herself back to take him faster but after squeezing her hips harder, she stopped trying to force him.

Dropping her forehead down, she breathed. He needed this. He'd take her hard and fast like she wanted, but first he had to have this reconnection.

Deliberately keeping his pace unhurried, he gritted his teeth as her warm cunt engulfed him. When he was finally fully buried inside, he rested his head on her shoulder.

"I love you," he whispered.

"My love, my mate," she responded softly.

That was what he needed to hear. Lifting his chest, he braced his knees and feet and started to withdraw.

Then plunged back.

Over and over again.

The slap of skin on skin and their cries filled the air around them. It was a heady sound. Picking up his rhythm, Jace continued to drive himself forward, claiming what was his.

Too soon and yet at the perfect moment, he felt the first twinge of release.

Lifting his right hand from Piper's hip, he clutched at her long hair and tugged her head back. Not enough to hurt but where he could watch her face.

She sobbed just as her inner muscles clamped down on his cock. He thrust hurriedly as she fell over the edge before finally following her over.

He came hard, shouting her name.

* * * *

There were sweats in one of the dresser drawers. Piper's body was pleasantly sore and felt well used.

Just walking past the spot on the floor where Jace had claimed her had her flushing. She still had a gut-burning desire to have another go at him but that would have to wait. She was starving and he needed to check on Mitch and Bobby.

Once they were dressed and she'd found a rubber band to pull her hair back, Jace opened the door and peeked out. She waited until he'd glanced back at her and nodded before following behind him.

Brian was leaning against the opposite wall. Piper had dozens of questions she was dying to ask him and knew Jace had just as many. The biggest shock had been learning that he was like her. He was obviously still in the military and from the sound of things, so were several others here. Just what in the hell was going on there?

"Mitch and Bobby just headed down the hall into the break room. I had the food put there if you're ready to join them," Brian explained as she and Jace exited the room.

She twined her fingers through Jace's when he reached for her. Since Jace didn't say anything, she remained silent also. Brian turned and they followed behind him.

She could hear Bobby's voice carrying to her and immediately felt better. For some reason she just couldn't stand the thought of either Mitch or Bobby being too far from her.

Just outside the entrance, Brian stopped and stepped to the side. He dropped his gaze to the ground. The move seemed instinctual, and Piper had the urge to lay her hand over Brian's in some sort of acknowledgment. Instead she strolled past him, ignoring the heavy sigh she heard.

Piper was relieved to see Mitch looking better. He sat at a table with an empty plate in front of him. From the scent, she would guess he'd just finished a steak.

"Smells good," she commented, walking up to them.

Bobby jumped up and hugged her. She returned the embrace before clasping Mitch on the shoulder. "You okay?"

"Much better now that I've eaten," he replied.

"Here, sit and I'll make you a plate." Bobby held out a chair.

"Thanks, but I can serve myself. Finish your meal," she ordered gently.

Bobby was underweight and she hadn't had a lot of time to work on that. She'd have to make sure she made it a priority.

Seated at the table across from Bobby was Cody. She nodded politely but didn't say anything. She didn't trust the guy and it was all she could do not to snarl at him until he was far away from her men. The feelings were overwhelming but she knew it had something to do with them belonging to her.

Vince's last words had been to call her an Alpha. How he'd known, she wasn't certain.

Luckily it appeared Jace either hadn't heard or didn't remember. Now that they were away from Vince, she was reluctant to confess like she'd been planning. So much had happened. The thought of losing Jace was enough to make her ill.

Having a Pack, her being an Alpha... What if he couldn't handle it?

Jace patted her lower back as he moved to his own chair. No one said anything while they piled their plates with meat, potato salad, slaw and soft, buttery rolls.

Once they'd had enough to get started, Jace nodded at Brian. "Have you eaten?"

Brian just shook his head.

"Will you join us?" Jace requested.

Moving quickly, Brian sat on the other side of Jace and began loading up. Piper took a big bite of the juicy steak and almost moaned. *Damn, this is good.*

She tried a little bit of the side dishes and could have wept that her neglected stomach was finally being satisfied.

Half her food was gone before she slowed down. Once she did, she glanced around the table. Jace and Brian were shoveling their meal in just as quickly as she had. Mitch was going to town on another plateful while Cody and Bobby just watched everyone else.

Catching her eye, Jace smiled and paused in eating. He nodded toward Brian then lifted his eyebrow. She caught on to what Jace wanted.

Setting her fork down, she looked over the soldier. He was an attractive man, about the same age as Jace. While her mate had never mentioned him before, through their bond she could feel how much Jace wanted to trust him.

"How long have you been different, Brian?" she asked, as a way of starting the questioning Jace was anxious to get to. She still wasn't sure what to call their transformations.

Startled eyes jumped up to meet her gaze. "Uh..." He paused long enough to wipe his mouth with a paper napkin. "Well, as you can see, I wasn't killed in action."

Jace snorted.

"I was attacked. Since at the time we didn't know what being changed meant, everyone in my unit was reported dead."

"And now?" Jace pressed.

"Now I lead a special division that is researching what we are. I have been able to take my experience in Intelligence and gain more knowledge of what has happened to us."

Jace and Mitch exchanged a look that she couldn't read. Although she didn't know what the two men were thinking, she could feel their wariness through the bond.

"Maybe you should start from the beginning," Jace suggested.

"Yeah," Brian agreed. "So my unit was charged with finding insurgents in the Afghan mountains. Rumors had been circulating for several weeks about a high-powered leader returning. We were dropped in at night and had forty-eight hours to get all the intel possible."

As Brian leaned back in his chair, settling into his story, Piper poured more coffee. She was existing on fumes and needed to keep sharp.

"At first everything went as any other op. We stayed silent and hidden, moving from one tribe to another. As the sun started to come up, we noticed more and more excitement in the villages but we could never catch the name or names of who was bringing on the activity."

Brian glanced at Jace. "You understand what I'm saying. How frustrating it is to know something was happening but couldn't find any clue."

After Jace nodded his agreement, Brian seemed to relax even more into his story. Piper couldn't imagine having to live through what the men around her had. They'd sacrificed so much for so little reward. They believed in helping others and had committed their lives to that goal.

"We moved as much as we could during the day. We had to remain unseen and finally decided to split up. Three of us took the south and I sent my other three teammates to the north. Then it started to get dark."

Jace shuddered, and Piper wondered how reliving this story would affect him. She wished she was close enough to offer some comfort. Instead all she could do was remain silent and listen to the man. Well maybe not just sit there, she closed her eyes and breathed deeply. She found the bond to Jace easily and just started to send her feelings toward him. He loved him, he was a strong man, and she would be lost without him. Love, affection and respect, she pushed those words toward him. She heard him gasp and reopened her eyes. He glanced at her and smiled. Hopefully she helped. She felt better for trying anyway.

"Finally after the sun set, the men and women started to make their way deep into the mountains. We followed and couldn't believe what we saw. It wasn't a person but a large Pack of wolves."

Piper could guess where the rest of the story was headed.

"Watching those people shift and transform for the first time was terrifying. By the time they'd turned into their second forms, it was too late. They easily picked up our scent."

The pain in Brian's voice was too much for Piper to ignore. She stood and quickly walked over to where he was seated. Placing her hand against the back of his neck, she breathed deeply.

The change in Brian was immediate. The tension in his muscles relaxed and he slumped forward. Since she wasn't sure exactly what she'd done except following instinct, she glanced at Jace, confused.

He nodded slightly while smiling.

"That's amazing," Brian murmured.

"Can you finish or do you need a break?" Jace questioned quietly.

"I'm good," Brian assured them, although he did press his neck harder against Piper's palm. "They were organized and relentless," Brian continued. "While we did manage to take out several, their numbers were too great. Eventually we all fell."

Rubbing her thumb across Brian, Piper regretted not being able to do more.

"I thought I was dead when the wolf bit down on my shoulder. I passed out from the pain and knew it was the end — only it wasn't," Brian told them. "I woke in a dark cave in the most intense pain I'd ever felt. I could see some of the other members of my unit. That was when they started to change us."

"How long did they have you?" Mitch asked.

"Six days. We missed our pick-up and they sent another unit in to find us — or what happened to us. The transformations were complete but we knew we'd never be able to hide what had happened."

"How many were changed?" she asked with dread.

"Four, but more know about us. Six in my unit and two of our bosses. I don't know how far up the knowledge has gotten."

It was so much to take in. After patting Brian's shoulder one last time, Piper went back to take her seat. Instead, Jace caught her hand as she passed him and pulled her onto his lap.

"We've been setting up the new unit ever since we returned. I knew about Cody's experience from reports and visited with him a few times. So when he called and told me about the three of you being captured, I knew I had to do something."

"We're grateful," Piper said sincerely. "You didn't know about Vince?"

"I tried to speak with him several times but he kept dodging me. It wasn't until Cody called him over without telling him I would show up, that I finally cornered him. That was last week."

"What happened?" Piper questioned.

"Nothing. He told me a story about being turned during leave and stated he didn't know who changed him. I didn't believe him but I couldn't call him out just yet. So we followed him for a few days and that is how we knew about the building."

"I didn't know what to do," Bobby spoke up. "Mitch made me hide when those guys came up to the room. After he was taken, I waited to see if you would come back. I was sure you would."

"It's okay," Piper assured him.

"You did the right thing, Bobby," Jace agreed. "It was smart going to Cody for help."

"I didn't know how to really help," Cody added. "I called Brian and let him know that you'd asked to meet with Vince."

"We followed you to the bar that night. Sadly we didn't see you leave the next day. We had a meeting with our superiors and missed Vince disappearing. We didn't put it together that you'd be in danger. We figured you went back home when Cody didn't hear from you again," Brian said.

Wow, anything could have changed what happened to them. If Brian's people had been watching, they might have gotten out sooner. Mitch would still be human.

"I wish we'd have known," she said sadly. "But again, thank you for the rescue."

Brian's gaze met hers. "Now that we've met, I have to believe that it was meant to be. My team was fated to rescue you."

Piper tensed. "What do you mean?"

"I'm a pretty strong wolf, but we know that no one in our unit is an Alpha."

Uncomfortable, Piper gripped Jace's hand. No, this couldn't be happening. She'd decided to wait on telling Jace. She glanced over at Bobby and saw his face had paled. "And?" she pressed.

"We need you."

"Need me to do what?"

"Become our Alpha. Accept us into your Pack. We've gotten no help from anyone we've come across. Instead, they have shunned us. We don't know much, but more and more information is being uncovered. Still, we can feel something missing."

"Missing?" Jace asked what Piper was afraid to. "And what do you mean about Piper being your Alpha?"

"We're military. We need a leader, and our wolves need a guide. Piper is such a strong lycan that she'd easily be able to give us what we need."

"I don't…" Jace paused to peer over at her.

She dropped her chin. This wasn't how she wanted him to find out. Hell, she hadn't wanted him to find out at all.

"Piper?"

She had to force herself to meet his gaze.

Jace gasped. "You knew?"

Unable to help glancing over at Bobby, she remained silent.

"Bobby?" Jace practically growled.

"I knew after the first time I shifted with her. I was compelled to submit to her."

"You… That's what was wrong when you both came back to us all that time ago," Jace accused.

"It's not like that. I just needed time to think about it," Piper told him.

Jace stood. He was clenching his jaw, and anger flashed in his eyes. "We need to discuss this in private."

He didn't wait for her to respond, just turned on his heel and stomped out of the room.

"I'm sorry. I thought he knew. It's not liking you were hiding it," Brian told her.

"How did you know?" she asked suspiciously.

"You forced Mitch—a newly turned, deeply wounded wolf—to transform. Only his Alpha would have been able to do that."

"I don't know anything. You've probably learned more than I have."

"We can offer you our intel and you can offer us a Pack. Talk to Jace. I'll hang around in case you have any more questions, but we need you. I think you just might need us as much."

* * * *

Jace wasn't sure what to say to Piper. She'd entered the room quietly and not moved away from the door. She looked at him with sympathy, her eyes bright with unshed tears. He didn't want to make her feel that way but he couldn't help the anguish he felt at her keeping things from him.

"Why didn't you tell me?" he asked.

She opened her mouth but shook her head.

"You keep secrets from me now? What else haven't you told me? I thought we were partners, mates, but…"

"We are," she whispered.

"Then why?" he demanded.

"How much more can you take?" she cried. "When are you going to decide enough is enough? I can't lose you! Don't you understand that? If you left me…"

Jace hadn't been prepared for the tears. "Oh, baby."

She tried to push him away, but Jace wasn't having any of that.

Embracing her, he held her tight. "I could never leave you. I don't know why you would think that."

"I tell myself you won't, but I know that without you, I don't have anything. I love you so much."

"I love you too. God, Piper, you're everything to me. You have to trust me."

"I'm so scared everything that is happening will end up driving you away. I got you kidnapped, tortured and your best friend turned."

"Well, see? I thought I got you kidnapped, tortured and my best friend turned. I was the one that pushed for you to learn more about yourself. I had Mitch call Cody and requested to meet with Vince."

"It's not your fault," Piper told him.

"Neither is it yours," he pointed out.

Piper sniffled before laughing quietly. "What a pair we make!"

"Yeah," he agreed before leading her to the bed. "We need to talk about what this means."

She sighed but settled next to him. "I'm scared."

"I know."

Chapter Fifteen

Piper crawled back into bed with her mind still whirling. The shower had helped ease her tense muscles and had given her time to clear her mind.

Jace was warm and welcoming as she cuddled close.

She didn't want to think any more about anything. How had her life come to staying at a Marine Corps base as werewolves tried to get her to become their Alpha?

"How are you holding up?" he asked quietly, rolling over to wrap his arm around her.

"I don't know what to do," she admitted.

"Shh, don't think about it right now. Rest. We'll have plenty of time to come to a decision," he told her.

As she closed her eyes, she tried to blank her mind. Jace's lips softly on the back of her neck helped pull her away from her thoughts. Grateful for his love and support, Piper twined her fingers with his where his hand rested on her stomach.

All she needed was Jace. Everything else would be okay.

* * * *

The strong scent of freshly mowed grass teased her senses as Piper leaped over one of the other wolves. She barely managed to stop another from side bumping her.

Rolling out of the way, she easily bounded back up on her four paws.

It felt good running with her Pack. Instead of the constant worry she usually had when in her animal form, she was free. Able to play and fool around out in the open with no fear of discovery.

Even in wolf form she knew who the others around her were. Mitch, Bobby and Brian stayed at her side the entire time. Spread out farther, more wolves danced around, and while she didn't know their names, there was a strong bond.

They were all hers.

Well, hers and Jace's. No longer strangers but family and friends. Each member of the Pack filled a hole that Piper hadn't even been aware she'd had.

An enticing aroma floated through the air, bringing her to a stop. Her mate.

Turning her head, she spotted her man standing just outside the field that she and the others were currently playing in. Throwing her head back, she howled for him.

One lone call turned louder as each Pack member joined her calling to the Alpha male.

The link burned bright between her and Jace. The minute he started toward her, she could feel his attention deep within her heart.

Jogging toward him, she kept her gaze locked on his. Jace didn't fear her in this form. Instead love and admiration came through their connection.

Piper bumped against his leg until he knelt to bury his hands into her fur. Within a couple of minutes, they were surrounded by the others.

A happy sound escaped as she accepted the warmth of her people.

* * * *

Since Jace wasn't yet awake, Piper quietly climbed out of bed. Usually he was always up before her but he needed rest. The dream had been so vivid that she actually felt more refreshed than she could have imagined.

On silent feet, she tiptoed to the door and exited without making a sound.

She wasn't surprised when she spotted Brian leaning against the wall across from her door. His head was tilted back while he snored.

Keeping watch. It wasn't necessary but she appreciated the gesture, especially with Mitch still recovering.

Not wanting to disturb him either, she slowly made her way to the room next to hers. Tapping on the door, she hoped Bobby would hear her. She didn't want to just walk in.

Luckily the door opened and Bobby peered up at her.

"Hey," she whispered.

He smiled brightly before waving her inside.

Mitch was in one of the beds covered up while watching her enter.

"How are you feeling?" she asked concerned.

"Hungry," Mitch told her.

Laughing, she nodded in understanding. "I know. If you get up, we'll see about getting some breakfast."

"I was just dreaming about pancakes."

Seeing Mitch in good spirits relieved some of her worry. She turned toward Bobby. "How about you?"

His shrugging in answer wasn't going to fly.

Mitch frowned at Bobby. "Why don't I jump in the shower and then we'll go eat? Jace still asleep?"

"Yeah but he'll probably be up soon."

"Okay, give me a few minutes."

Piper waited until Mitch had the water started before sitting on Mitch's bed. Waving across from her, she motioned for Bobby to sit.

When Bobby was settled, she leaned forward. "Talk to me. Tell me how you are feeling."

"I can't help but feel responsible. Every time I look at Mitch, I know it's my fault he was turned."

"How is it your fault?" she asked.

"If I was strong enough to fight, he wouldn't have been taken. Instead I hid like a little boy."

"You stayed safe so you could bring in the troops and rescue us. We're the ones that contacted Vince," she assured him. Dropping down to her knees in front of him as she gripped his hands, she made certain his gaze met hers. "You did good. I am so proud of you."

"Really?" he asked tentatively.

"I swear."

"Thanks. Mitch said the same thing but I just couldn't believe him. How is he not mad at me?"

"Because it's not your fault. If I have to tell you all day, every day, until you believe me, I will."

Bobby's chuckle was low but heartfelt. "I'll work on it."

Piper squeezed his hands before getting back on the bed. Curling her legs under her, she looked closely at him. "So Cody came through."

She expected the blush.

"Yeah, he was pretty great," Bobby agreed.

"You like him?"

Bobby chewed on his lip instead of answering as he glanced away.

"It's okay if you do," she told him.

Bobby's gaze came back to her quickly. "I didn't think you liked him."

"I don't know him, but he did get Brian. If you like him then I'll make an effort to talk with him," she promised.

"I just feel a connection to him. Like maybe he understands me," Bobby confided.

"That's good."

"I don't know if he feels the same, though."

"You have time. Make the effort to learn more about him. Jace and I will be here to support you."

"Is Jace mad?"

"No, he was upset that I'd kept a big secret from him, but he also understood. You can't put that on yourself either. I made the decision not to share my concern with Jace. We'll get past this. We love each other too much not to." Piper believed what she was saying.

She'd hurt Jace and she know knew that she would have to learn from her mistake. She'd never hide anything from him again. She trusted him to stand by her. He deserved her faith in him.

"Thanks, Piper."

"You're welcome."

The water shut off but that was okay. She felt good about her talk with Bobby. Now they needed to fuel up. Hopefully things could start to settle down.

* * * *

Jace woke slowly, breathing in Piper's fresh and clean scent, knowing she was safe and sound, even if she wasn't in bed with him.

Glancing at his watch, he noted it was just after eight in the morning. He normally never slept so late, but he'd needed it.

The emotional drain from the last few days had started to catch up with him. His heart-to-heart with Piper the night before had also helped to settle the unease inside.

He'd known that she wasn't sharing everything with him. He should have pressed her but at the time, he hadn't known what they were dealing with.

Piper was an Alpha among her people—a leader that others would depend on. While he knew she was up for the job, she still doubted herself. He was relieved to see that she was at least open to speaking with Brian. Of learning more. Hopefully she'd gotten enough rest to decide how they should proceed. Jace wanted to go home.

He'd find her and they could start to make plans. He climbed out of bed and dressed quickly. He strolled to the door and yanked it open intent on tracking her down. He was surprised to see Brian outside the door again. Didn't the guy ever sleep?

"Good morning," Brian greeted him.

"Hey, how are you?" he asked. It was still strange to be talking with the man he'd thought was dead.

Smiling brightly, Brian looked good. "I'm great, actually."

Well, that was an unexpected answer. "Really?" he questioned.

"I know you don't understand completely about Piper's shifter status, but just having her here has gone a long way to calming me. This morning as I made sure breakfast was ordered, I just enjoyed being in the same room with her. Have you spoken about her taking the position of Alpha?"

Shaking his head, Jace wasn't sure how to respond. "About that, we need to talk."

"Sure, how about some coffee? The others have started breakfast."

"Please." Jace really needed the caffeine. He followed Brian to the same small room that they'd had dinner in the previous night.

He quickly greeted Piper and the others, glad to see them settling in.

The smell of freshly brewed coffee was heaven. Set out on one side of the room in buffet style were silver covered dishes. Ignoring the food for now, he headed straight to the table with coffee pots and juice containers.

He poured two mugs before he carried them over to sit beside Brian.

"I'm sorry I never told you I was still alive. When I came back from the mission, I was so fucked up and scared that I just went with anything the brass said. I really thought they'd end up killing us all."

Jace could understand. He'd thought long and hard the night before about how he would have handled being turned during his time in service.

In all honesty, he probably wouldn't have done anything different from Brian. "I don't blame you. It's just taking some time for me to get used to. I thought you were dead. What are the chances that not only are you sitting here with me but you also share the same secret as the woman I love?"

"Fate works in mysterious ways," Brian commented quietly.

"Fate?" he scoffed.

Grinning, Brian only looked back at him. "You said it yourself. What are the chances?"

"We're here, so what's next?"

Setting his cup on the table, Brian turned in his chair to face Jace directly. "That depends on you and Piper."

He didn't even pretend not to understand what Brian was talking about. Glancing over at Piper, he saw she'd stopped eating. "You were serious? You want Piper to become the Alpha of your unit?"

Brian was already nodding before Jace had even finished his question. "We have the resources to investigate our kind all over the world—to get answers that we need. We'll do that, but we still need you both. We crave the structure of a Pack. We have to have an Alpha."

"I understand wanting Piper as your Alpha, but why do you need me?"

"It's hard to explain. I'm drawn to Piper."

Jace narrowed his eyes at Brian.

Laughing while waving his hand at Jace, Brian was obviously amused. "Not that way. She's a beautiful woman but I don't want to sleep with her."

The protectiveness he felt toward Piper eased at Brian's admission. He believed his old buddy.

"While I crave Piper claiming me as one of her Pack, I also feel the desire to submit to you."

"What?"

"You're a part of Piper. Her mate, and we can feel the bond. We yearn for your acceptance also. The Alpha male to us."

"I feel the same way," Bobby offered. "I have from the start."

Sitting back in his chair, Jace thought about Brian and Bobby's statements. He already felt a connection with Bobby, and he hadn't known the young man long. Was it because of his link with Piper?

"I have a question," Piper spoke up.

Brian nodded, appearing relaxed and willing to answer.

"Vince didn't figure out I was an Alpha but you picked it up just because I forced Mitch to change?"

"I also met you in your shifted form. Your power is even stronger when you transform. I have no idea what we would have done if you'd been on the other side of things. It could have ended badly for us," Brian answered.

Piper glanced over at him, seeming to accept Brian's explanation. Worry was etched in her delicate features, though, and Jace wasn't sure how he could help. He'd find some way, though.

"What exactly do you want of us?" Jace asked directly.

"Most of what we know is instinct. I wish I had all the answers for you. But having you close calms me. I think it will be the same with the others. They've already asked, and I told them I'd arrange for them to meet Piper officially when she was ready."

"How would Piper becoming your Alpha work?"

"Our commander is aware of you and Piper. I also updated him on the events of yesterday. I mentioned Mitch and Bobby, so they are welcome here with you. Since Mitch is still active, he is being transferred under my command. You, Piper and Bobby will have full access to our base at all times."

"Access?"

"We still must serve, but I think if we have contact with Piper, we'll be able to handle our missions better. Right now our duties are all stateside, but that could change. We have enough leeway that as we figure out what we require, all we have to do is ask."

"The government is backing you up without...experimenting on you or anything?" Jace asked, knowing that was one of Piper's biggest fears.

With Brian squirming in his chair, Jace immediately tensed up. "What?"

"They did run some tests on us when we first came back but it isn't *us* that they are *experimenting* on."

"What does that mean?"

"Well, they did capture some of the men who turned us."

"You can't torture and test on others. It's not right," Piper demanded.

"That's what I think, but I don't make those decisions. That is way past my pay grade. All I know is that every month I get an update on what they're told or find out. It's the way things work."

Leaning forward, he gripped Brian's shoulder. "Okay, we'll figure something out. Piper's right, though. We won't be a part of anyone being experimented on."

Brian's gaze strayed to Mitch. "I can understand that."

"Will you consider our offer, at least?" Brian asked.

"We'll choose together. All of us," Piper stated firmly.

Love flowed through him. Even though he wanted to know what was happening with her and the bond they shared, he just couldn't let anyone be tormented. Not that he would be able to tell anyone that either. He was a civilian.

"So I work with you now?" Mitch spoke up.

"Yes, we'll get the paperwork finalized but for now, you're on leave. You can stay at your place or live on base."

"Right now I think it would be best if Mitch returned home with us," Jace answered Brian.

Mitch was nodding in agreement.

"That's fine. Like I said, you'll be able to get on base at any time. Their barracks haven't been used in years, so we've made them ours. They needed some improvement but I think we're good for now."

"I don't know what I'll want to do yet. If I'll even re-enlist when I come up. But I do want to stay with Jace and Piper for a while," Mitch told Brian.

Jace studied Mitch as he pushed the food around on his plate. His best friend was still a little pale but was also looking much better this morning. He stood to get his own food. Jace nudged Mitch as he walked past him and grinned when Mitch bumped him back.

It took a few minutes for him to fill his plate and when he returned, the conversation had changed to where Bobby would live.

He scooted his chair as close as possible to Piper's and made sure their legs were touching. "Piper's right, Bobby. We have more than enough room," Jace told the young man.

"I don't want to impose," Bobby argued.

"You won't be," Jace replied easily.

"Maybe for a little bit," Bobby finally agreed. "But I do need to get my own place and decide what to do. I haven't even been home since the attack. I don't want to return to Arizona, but I would like to finish school."

"Then we'll see that you do," Piper told him. "As soon as we get back to the house, we'll start planning. One of us can go home with you too, and get anything you need. Help take care of things."

Bobby nodded eagerly. "Yes, please. I would appreciate the help."

"It's settled then. Marcus can run the bar for a little longer. It's why I hired him." Jace was happy with the direction they were going in.

"So what do you want to do now?" Brian asked the group.

"First we should probably meet with your people. If we are going to do this, we need to work out when we'll come down to the base. Luckily we're not far away and we can even have some gatherings at our home. I would like to return as soon as possible, though."

"Of course," Brian agreed.

"Let us get ready and talk things over, and we'll see what we need to do," Jace told him.

"I'll see if my captain is available. He'll want to talk to you."

"Set it up," Jace ordered, before turning to Piper. "Ready?"

* * * *

"Are you sure about this?" Jace had to ask Piper. They'd returned to their room and Piper seemed okay with staying longer and working with Brian.

"I am. I had a dream last night and it felt like a sign. It's almost like this is the most natural step."

"Can you believe a week ago you didn't even want to shift?" he asked, still finding the events that had led them there crazy.

"No, it seems like a lifetime ago. We've changed so much."

"We're closer, though. Still together. We have Bobby and Mitch and maybe others."

"I'd...like to help," she replied quietly. "Not just to get what information we can about them, but I remember being so lost. No one would help me. I can't do that to someone else."

Jace stepped over to the bed, cupping her face. "Your big heart is one of the reasons I love you. You'll be a great leader."

Piper laughed nervously. "I don't know how good I'll be, but I can't *not* try."

Hearing the anxiety, he bent to kiss her. "I know this will work," Jace said when he pulled away.

"Let's do this then." Piper stood. "Shall we meet our Pack?"

* * * *

Jace shook hands with Brian's commander, Captain Jeffery Williams. The older man smiled widely as he pumped Jace's hand. "Ms. Maxwell." Captain Williams waved Piper forward. "It is a pleasure to meet you. I'm thrilled you've agreed to take over the Pack."

She glanced over at Jace before she laid her palm into the captain's. The touch was brief, and since she showed no reaction, Jace knew that Williams was indeed human.

"I will try to do my best for everyone involved," Piper told him.

"That's all we can ask. I wanted to welcome you both and assure you that the full support of the Armed Forces are at your disposal. Please, have a seat."

The office of the commander, while large, had a somewhat homey feeling to it. As Jace settled onto one of the plush brown couches, he pulled Piper down by his side.

"Any questions you might have, I'll try to answer," Captain Williams told them as he sat in the leather chair across from them. "While Brian will be your main contact for anything military, my door is always open."

"We appreciate that," Jace replied sincerely. "I guess our first question is, what exactly do you expect from us…from Piper?"

"I'll be the first to admit that I don't know a thing about being a shifter or what is required. I chose Brian to be in charge of the shifters since he was the most qualified and from his personal experience. He believes his new…Pack…needs an Alpha. With Piper's connection to you and your excellent military record, I agreed Piper would be the best fit. Other than that, I can't really tell you what will be required. I just don't know."

At least Captain Williams was honest, Jace mused, as he nodded at the captain's words.

"I believe that Brian explained you would have full access to this part of the base. While the common areas and barracks have been closed for many years prior to us opening them back up, we do have the resources to expand on the buildings if needs be."

"This all sounds very nice but…" Piper started before looking over at Jace.

"We're trying to figure out what the catch is," Jace provided for her.

Piper slipped her hand into his, and he gave her a reassuring squeeze.

Since he'd fucked up the last time, he'd thought he could get her answers. Jace had to make sure that the government was on the up and up. He could not—*would not*—let anyone else harm her. But he felt deep down that this was what they were supposed to do.

"There is no catch. We need to protect the men and women that we send out in the name of freedom. To do that, Brian tells me the Pack must be stable and healthy. We need Piper to give them the unity they crave."

"We start on a trial basis," Jace told him. "We'll give it three months. After that, Piper will decide whether or not she wants to continue. If we choose to walk away at that point, you will allow us."

Captain Williams was already nodding. "Yes, yes that is good."

Jace glanced over at Piper. He could feel the link that connected them tugging. She was okay.

Chapter Sixteen

Piper and Jace walked with their fingers twined together, as Mitch and Bobby joked around in front of them making Piper grin like a fool. "I think this is a good idea," she told Jace.

Letting Mitch shift out in the open for the first time seemed right. As soon as Piper had brought it up, Mitch had gotten so excited. If he had already been in shifted form, his tail would have been wagging, she'd wager.

They wanted to give Mitch a little alone time before the others gathered. Piper had decided that the best way to approach the group would be to see how they ran together.

Wasn't that what her dream had been about? Since she was only going on instinct, she hoped she was right about this bringing them close quickly.

It was great to see Mitch getting some of his bounce back.

Bobby laughed before jumping on Mitch's back. Mitch groaned playfully before his laughter boomed across the empty field.

"They look like puppies." Piper stopped walking, drawing Jace to a halt also.

Jace was chuckling while shaking his head.

Mitch fell to the ground, taking Bobby with him. They rolled playfully and indeed looked childlike — or puppy-like.

"Let's get ready to transform," Bobby said to Mitch after they'd worn themselves out.

Mitch glanced over to where Piper stood watching. "You sure I should do this here?"

She nodded. "It should make you feel better."

"I'll keep watch, but I'm sure it will be okay," Jace assured him.

Piper turned back to Jace, they were really lucky to have him on their side. All of them were. "Thank you," she said softly. When she started to pull away, he wrapped his arms tightly around her back to hold her in place and kissed her thoroughly.

As their tongues met, stroked, she lost herself to the sensations. It wasn't until she heard Mitch groaning in complaint did she pull away.

Face flushing, she was panting after Jace released her. "Mmm," she practically purred at him.

Jace's smile was wicked.

She was reluctant to leave his side but she also was looking forward to Mitch's first transformation since their release.

Bobby had been the only other one she'd run with and that experience had been great.

"Let's get started," she called out.

Of course that got their attention. Bobby removed his shirt quickly, dropping the garment on the ground without care. It would easier for Mitch to concentrate if he wasn't worried about getting tangled in his clothes. She followed suit, trying not to think about the fact she was getting naked in front of two men plus her mate.

If their little group grew, she would have to think about that some more.

Nodding first to Bobby, she then held her hand out to Mitch.

She spoke low, walking Mitch through the same steps as she had with Bobby the first time.

"Picture your wolf. He's big and beautiful. Powerful and ready to come out. Close your eyes and just let the feeling flow over you."

Mitch's body seemed to relax just as he started to copy her movements. They knelt, moved onto all fours, and the transformation began.

Jace made sure he stayed in the same spot as the three people who meant the most to him in the world changed from human to wolf.

It didn't surprise him that Mitch was the slowest to shift. He had the most to learn.

Within minutes, Piper shook her entire body as she tended to do at the beginning of every run. Mitch copied her but his dark gaze was fixed on Piper.

She loped over, brushing against Mitch like Jace had seen her do with Bobby.

The three wolves rubbed and licked each other before Piper separated herself.

Her gait was slow as she made her way to his side. Burying his hand in the scruff of her neck, he stroked and massaged. As he loved on his mate, Bobby and Mitch went back to bowling over one another and nipping gently.

Piper's weight against his side was solid as they watched their friends together.

Kneeling down, he cupped her muzzle. "Go, have fun. I will be right here."

One rough sweep of her tongue against his check and she was gone, leaping into the fray and knocking the two male wolves down.

Jace sat where he was, not willing to break his promise to Piper. He wouldn't move an inch.

Chuckling as he watched Mitch try to leap over Bobby but not clearing him, Jace enjoyed the show.

Piper had once told him that it had taken a while to get use to walking on four legs instead of two.

He'd assumed that changing into the wolf would aid them and he guessed to a certain point it did, but he was finding out that not everything he'd assumed was correct. Some things, though, were instinct. Piper had that already. She had it in her to lead. All she had to do was believe. He would do what he could to help also.

Hearing faint footsteps behind him, he turned his head, spotting Brian cautiously making his way toward him.

"Hey," Jace greeted him quietly.

"I don't want to interrupt but just wanted to make sure you all had everything you needed."

Glancing back at the three wolves playing before returning his gaze to Brian, Jace grinned. "I think we're good."

"Okay," Brian said as he rolled from the tip of his feet and back.

Getting the distinct impression that Brian really didn't want to leave, Jace patted the ground to his right. "Pull up some grass."

A look of such relief passed over Brian's features that Jace's heart squeezed. Brian sat down before stretching his legs out. "They look like they're having fun."

"I think so," Jace agreed. "They needed this. Mitch hasn't been able to shift just for the joy of it."

"Yeah, I can't believe he was turned."

"There's a lot that I can't believe," Jace stated with a tinge of sadness. "Like two of my best friends being werewolves."

Chuckling, Brian shook his head. "You have a point."

"How do you think it will go tonight?" Jace asked his friend.

"I think good. With a group this small, Piper is all anyone can talk about—even the humans."

"I'm still not sure what you expect her to do."

Brian gazed out at the field. "Just what she is doing there. Uniting us."

He caught Piper nip Bobby teasingly. "We'll find out shortly, I guess."

Wow! The pleasure of running and teasing two Pack mates was more fun than Piper would have ever imagined.

Mitch remained more standoffish, not quite as secure on four paws as her and Bobby, but that was okay. He would gain confidence. She had no doubt.

Bobby grew friskier the longer the three of them remained in shifted form. She even had to calm him down so he wouldn't knock Mitch over. It was actually strange that she could be in her wolf form out in the open. Back at home she was so scared of being found out. On base, they didn't have to hide.

Not to say that she didn't maintain awareness of her surroundings. She made sure that Jace was in sight while the area around them remained empty. Brian had said he'd take care to ensure they wouldn't be disturbed, and Piper was glad the man had kept his word.

Later they would shift again. However, the group would be bigger.

At least they would find out quickly whether or not her being Alpha would work. If they had any trouble tonight, she could still back out.

Bobby bumped her side, drawing her attention back to the present. There was time to decide what to do later. Right now she was going to enjoy her time in her other form.

* * * *

"Wow," Piper said to Brian. "I don't really know how to get started."

"They are just as curious about you as you are them. They want this to work. Just be yourself," Brian told her.

Sure, be herself. *That shouldn't be too hard?* Yeah right. Her hands were shaking while nerves tingled throughout her body.

She wasn't sure she was ready. Oh, she had the desire, but what if she completely fucked up and someone got hurt?

"You okay?" Jace whispered into her ear as he came up behind her.

They hadn't approached the group yet, so she let herself relax back into him while he wrapped his arms around her, and she smiled just a little. Part of her anxiety consisted of letting him down.

Jace believed that she could be Alpha. She'd do her very best not to let him down.

"You don't have to do this so soon."

Realizing that she hadn't answered him, Piper turned in his arms to gaze up at him. How had she gotten so lucky? Her mate was so handsome and strong. "It'll be okay. Just trying to get my bearings."

"You'll be great. I know you will," he said softly.

Rising onto the tips of her toes, she pressed her lips gently against his.

"Thank you for being here with me," she said against his lips.

"I wouldn't be anywhere else."

Hearing the restlessness of the people gathered, Piper gave Jace one more brief kiss before pulling away. She nodded at Brian to get things started before following him to be introduced.

Brian whistled sharply, gaining the attention of everyone in attendance. "As you know, we've been lucky enough to meet a few of my friends. I know most of you have heard the rumors about one of them being an Alpha. These are true. I'd like you to meet Piper Maxwell."

The round of applause and shouts that greeted her came as a big shock. Overwhelmed, she found herself taking a step back until Jace laid his palm on the small of her back.

Just that small contact was enough to give her strength. She smiled out at her Pack.

"Now, I know you all will have questions for her," Brian continued. "There will be plenty of time to get to know not only your Alpha but also her mate and the two new members of our Pack."

Brian waved a hand toward Jace, Bobby and Mitch.

"First, let her get a chance to talk with each of you then we'll transform together." Brian turned toward her and bowed his head.

Walking forward, she went with instinct by laying her hand on Brian's neck. The spark under her fingertips jolted her but she didn't release him. "Thank you," she said quietly.

Brian gasped but straightened as she drew her hand away. "Your power, I can feel it," he murmured.

Not sure what he meant, she simply nodded. "As Brian said, I do want to get to know every one of you. To build a connection and our Pack," she said.

She couldn't resist one last glance over at her mate. Jace stood with his shoulders back, gazing straight at her.

Moving forward, she drew closer to the small group.

Holding out her hand to the tall muscular Spanish man, she kept direct eye contact with him.

"Alpha," he stated shakily before dropping to his knees.

The others quickly followed.

Respect, need and just a little tint of fear flowed from the young man as Piper breathed deeply. She repeated the same gesture, placing her palm at his neck. She had planned just to meet each person and shake their hands, but this greeting just felt right.

Inside, her wolf was content and calm.

"Please call me Piper," she told him. "What's your name?"

"Adam Light."

"I'm very pleased to meet you, Adam."

"The pleasure is mine," he stated firmly.

She patted his neck before she moved to the woman of the unit. She was younger, with pretty, long blonde hair.

Piper felt her shudder at the electric current between them when Piper cupped the back of her neck.

"Alpha Piper, my name is Katy."

"Hi, Katy, I'm glad to meet you also. And just Piper is fine."

"Thank you. Thank you, Piper."

The last two shifters she met were Chris and Kevin. She could already tell that they'd get along.

Once she'd made the way to every member of her now expanded Pack, she rejoined Jace and Brian at the front. Facing the crowd, she swept one last look over the gathered troops then nodded to Brian.

"Let's shift," Brian said loudly.

In a flurry of movement everyone started to undress. Piper reached over to grip Jace's wrist. She turned toward him as she dropped her head to lean against his chest. She just needed to take a moment. Emotions were battling to be released but she wanted to remain strong.

"You okay?"

"I feel good," she told him honestly.

With Jace's arms embracing her back to pull her even closer. Piper had to stomp down her excitement.

"I was so proud watching you," Jace whispered. "Are you ready to run with them?"

"Yeah, I think I am."

Jace stood in front of her while she undressed, not that it was that important since the others had already turned. Piper took her time handing her clothes to Jace before dropping down onto her knees.

She pictured the wolf taking over and let everything else go. Sharp pricks ran along her spine then she was shifting.

It wasn't easy to draw a breath as the throbbing started to fade away. Once she thought she had her breath back, she rose onto her legs, stretching her neck out, she howled to those around her.

The answering sound echoed through the bare field, sending tingles of excitement throughout her entire body. Yipping in happiness, she darted to join the wolves prowling the area.

Mitch stood off to one side so she ran over to him first. Dragging her muzzle across his chin, she made sure he was okay. He head-butted her playfully so Piper left him to race over to Bobby.

She was surprised to see Bobby already making friends. Two large wolves that were close to him seemed to be cautious but willing to engage in silly antics. Bobby crouched and fake attacked.

They responded the same.

Just as she reached Bobby, the dark tawny wolf—Adam, she believed from his scent—pounced. Bobby managed to duck, but Piper wasn't prepared and collided with the large male, sending both of them rolling.

The impact surprised her yet she easily rotated back onto her paws. Shaking her fur out, she glanced over at the one that had knocked into her.

He immediately dropped to his stomach and whined.

Oh, Oh! She rushed over and nudged Adam. He rolled onto his back, giving her access to his belly.

Piper didn't want him to feel bad. They were just playing around. She positioned her snout under his back so he would flip right side.

The male followed her direction. As he regained his feet, she licked around his mouth.

His tail started to wag quickly, and she knew they were okay. Bobby bounded up to her, hitting her side with some force.

Piper darted after him when he took off at a full run.

He was still faster than she was, but she could keep up with him pretty well.

Hearing the others behind them, Piper let herself enjoy the wind through her fur and the unity of the Pack.

She could get used to this feeling of being complete for the first time since she'd been changed.

Chapter Seventeen

Jace gripped Brian's hand in his as their gazes met. "We'll be back on Monday and spend a few days with the Pack."

"I look forward to it. Last night was so great. We couldn't have had a better start," Brian told him.

"Yeah, Piper was so worn out that she fell asleep as soon as her head hit the pillow."

Brian released his hand but grasped Jace's shoulder. "I know it hurt when you found out I was still alive. I just wanted you to know that there were a few people I wish I could have told and you were one of them. By the time I had any control over my life, six months had gone by since my funeral."

Jace didn't blame his old friend. "It's forgotten. I don't know what I would have done in your shoes. I'm just glad that you're okay and we get to see each other once again."

Laughing, Brian pulled him into a manly hug, pounding on his back. Hell, man, we're family now."

He grinned back at his buddy. "I guess we are."

They were still embracing when Piper joined them at the vehicle. "Am I interrupting?" she teased.

Jace and Brian broke apart, a little embarrassed. Piper pushed under his arm so Jace could hold her. "It was good to meet you, Brian. We'll see you in a few days."

"Thanks for everything, Piper."

They shared their own quick hug while Bobby and Mitch finally arrived. They exchanged goodbyes before climbing in the vehicle.

"Let's head home," Jace told the group.

"That sounds great," Piper agreed.

Pulling out of the lot, he headed down the old paved road to the exit they would use.

This part of the base was perfect for what Brian was doing. His unit had full access to get in and out but still had privacy from the thousands of other soldiers housed close by.

He felt good being back on his old stomping grounds. Even though he had retired so he could settle down, he'd been missing the action. After the week he'd just had he was once again ready to get back to his old life. He missed his bar and friends more than he would have thought.

Glancing in the rear-view mirror, he caught Piper's gaze. She smiled brightly at him.

Anything he'd been through was worth it to have Piper in his life.

* * * *

The drive went by quickly as Mitch and Bobby talked constantly, discussing the run the night before. As Jace pulled up in front of the house, Piper just couldn't help feeling relieved. As much as she'd enjoyed being with Brian and the other wolves as well as the conversation on the return trip, nothing beat being home.

Still in borrowed sweats, she couldn't wait to get dressed in her own clothes, although she preferred to wear one of Jace's old shirts when she lounged around the house.

Following Jace up the walk, she checked out the small shrubs and dying flowers that lined the sidewalk. Now that Bobby was interested in Cody, she planned to either get him to help with the garden or see if she could give Bobby an excuse to spend time with him.

Either way, hopefully soon her front yard would be close to a masterpiece like Cody's.

As Jace unlocked and pushed the door open, stale air flooded over her.

"I'll start airing out the house," Jace said, obviously picking up on the same scent.

"Dinner sound good?" Mitch offered.

"Yeah, thanks," Jace replied as Piper grunted in response.

"How about coffee?" Bobby suggested.

"I'm going to shower first," Piper told them. She should probably help but she craved standing under the full shower spray.

"Okay, baby." Jace kissed her quickly before moving to the living room window.

Fresh salt air blew in, causing her to smile. She was home.

Piper took in the pictures that were hanging on the wall as she strolled down the hall. Photos of Jace's friends and old teammates started from the living room going back toward the bedroom. Closer to their sleeping quarters, Piper paused at the one photo of her and Jace.

She'd resisted taking the picture and having it added to the others but Jace had insisted.

They'd been just coming out of the water, smiling and happy, Piper was glad to see it. Marcus, the cook from the bar, had captured the moment for them.

Now that she had Bobby and Mitch and the others at the base, maybe they would be able to add even more—family prints showing their connection.

She continued into the bedroom and didn't stop until she reached the bathroom entry. She turned on the shower letting the water warm up as she undressed. Once naked, using her hand she tested the water before climbing into the stall.

The hot water beat down on her shoulders causing her to moan in pleasure. Picking up the bar of soap she preferred, she quickly started to rub down her body.

"Mmm, it smells like you in here," Jace said, opening the glass door.

Startled, Piper jumped.

"Didn't hear me?" he teased, joining her.

She laughed while shaking her head, she had to admit she'd been so far in bliss she hadn't been aware of her surroundings.

"I don't know whether to be worried or not that you weren't thinking about me. I was picturing you naked and wet and had to join you."

He must have been thinking about her for a while by his hard-on. Wrapping her arms around his neck, she pulled him close. "Are you sure we should be doing this with Bobby and Mitch in the house?"

"They know we have sex, Piper."

Oh, she was aware. Jace was right, though. They were in their private bathroom inside the bedroom. Lots of distance between them.

Humming, Piper used her slick body to rub fully against him.

Jace gripped her hips before bending his head and covering her mouth with his. She opened her lips and let his tongue inside.

His spicy flavor exploded in her mouth. She moaned, letting him know how much she desired him. His cock brushed against her stomach so she reached down and took him in hand.

Jace broke the kiss to groan into her neck while she stroked him. "God, I never get tired of feeling you touch me."

She knew just how he felt. "Just touch?"

Before Jace could respond, Piper dropped to her knees.

"Ahh." Jace threw his hands against the tiled wall as Piper dipped her head and started to lick at the tip of his cock.

She opened wide and took his erection into her mouth, peeking up at him. She sucked deeply before she started a quick rhythm bobbing her head.

One of his hands fell onto her head as he gave himself over to her. His stiff cock felt good against her tongue. She paid close attention to the bottom of his mushroom head. She knew just how to get him to the edge.

"Stop, Piper!" Jace pleaded.

Instead she doubled her efforts.

"Baby!" Jace called before putting pressure on the hold he had on her hair.

She frowned up at him after she popped off.

"I want to be inside you," he told her.

Piper sure as hell wasn't going to argue with him. Grasping the hand he offered, she rose to her feet.

"Let's get out of here and to the bed first," he suggested.

"Okay," she agreed readily.

She turned the knobs off as Jace pushed the stall door open. He already had a towel in his hand when she exited.

"Thanks," she said, reaching for it.

"Nope, come here."

She stepped up to him as he wiped her down. His movements were quick and didn't really get most of the water off.

"Dry?" he asked tossing the towel onto the floor.

"Who cares," she replied, slipping her arms around his waist.

He kissed her again—deeply and with lots of tongue. The sloppy touch showed her how impatient he was. She thought about teasing him when he started to tug her toward the bedroom but she needed him just as badly.

They hit the doorframe since neither of them could take their hands off one another.

"Ow," Piper said, laughing.

"Sorry. Can't wait."

"What?" Piper floundered as Jace picked her up, before placing her on top of the dresser to his side.

He settled his hips between her thighs before gripping her hair to pull her head back.

"Fuck," he murmured then latched his lips on the sensitive skin of her neck.

She shivered as he nipped and sucked. "Yes," she hissed in approval. Reaching down, she caught his cock in her hand. "Take me, right here."

"Yeah."

Positioning himself at her entrance, Jace paused briefly. "Look at me."

Piper raised her gaze.

"I love you."

"I love you too," she told him, just as he slid inside her wet pussy.

They moaned together.

God, he filled her so well. Jace pulled out before slamming back inside. Her back hit the wall and she loved it.

"More," she demanded.

He yanked her down, closer to the edge, as he withdrew again.

As he plunged back inside, Piper saw stars with the need so intense. Jace thrust over and over until they were both panting and lost in each other and their passion.

Piper buried her face in Jace's chest as she climaxed, trying to stifle the sound. As soon as Jace started to fill her with his seed, she couldn't care anymore.

Dropping her head back, she cried out for her mate.

* * * *

Jace felt loose and relaxed as he followed Piper into the kitchen. She was wearing an old pair of jeans that hugged her ass perfectly. It was all he could do not to cup her bottom before dragging her back to the bedroom.

She was also wearing one of the first Anderson's Loft T-shirts that had softened and grown worn out. She was sexy as hell in his top.

"I think that's a great idea!" Bobby stated as they entered.

"What idea?" Jace asked, strolling to the fridge. "Damn, that smells remarkable."

The aroma of spicy Italian sauce filled the large area, making his stomach growl.

"Thanks. It'll be done in a few minutes. And I offered to go with Bobby to Arizona and pick up his stuff. That way neither of you has to miss work," Mitch said.

Jace glanced over at Piper. Since she was grinning and nodding, he turned back to his best friend. "That does sound like a good plan."

"We can leave late tomorrow and get a hotel down the coast. Bobby has never been down there and I thought it would be nice to hang out."

"Will you be back in time to go to the base with us?" Piper questioned.

"Of course," Bobby spoke up. He was practically bouncing in his seat. "We wouldn't miss that."

"I think it's a good idea," Jace told them as he passed out beers. "Bobby hasn't been able to enjoy a road trip and Mitch needs time to unwind." He wouldn't mind some alone time with Piper either.

He understood how Piper was feeling, though. She felt responsible for both men as their Alpha and wanted them close to keep an eye on them. He did too, although seeing Piper in full Alpha mode was turning him on and he didn't want an audience for that.

"It's a plan then," Mitch announced. "Now, let's eat!"

They set their drinks down before making a line to fix their plates. There was fresh garlic bread to go with the spaghetti and meatballs.

Once everyone was ready, they all sat together at the table. It was nice—the aroma hanging in the air while they dined on an awesome feast.

"I still think you should come to work at the bar," Jace told Mitch after finishing half his plate.

"I just might take you up on that offer one of these days," Mitch responded, pointing his fork in Jace's direction.

"I'd weigh like…six hundred pounds," Piper said with a laugh.

"It'd be worth it, though," Bobby added.

Mitch dropped his head back over his plate, but Jace could see the pleased smile on his face.

He wasn't joking, though. Now that Mitch's life had changed, it might be time for him to consider doing something else. Although Brian was still making his career work, even turned, it was possible for Mitch to do the same, but Jace kind of hoped that Mitch would be around more, especially with the whole turning furry thing.

Before his current visit, it had probably been nine months since he'd seen his friend. Of course, Mitch had been overseas for most of that but still, Jace had missed him. Maybe having Bobby there would help.

The younger man would need a lot of support coming up. He needed to figure out if he wanted to go back to school like he'd said, or Jace could even get him working at the bar if Bobby needed time off. Hell, Bobby could stay with them for free. He just wanted to watch over the kid.

Seeing him joke around with Mitch about their upcoming trip made his heart feel fuller.

Piper's hand landed on his knee and he realized he was staring at Bobby while lost in thought. He sent her a quick wink before returning to his meal. He needed to let Mitch and Bobby make their own decisions. He wasn't their dad, for fuck's sake.

* * * *

"Marcus!" Jace called out as he opened the front door to Anderson's Loft.

"Back here," came the muffled reply.

He exchanged amused looks with Piper before heading toward the kitchen. Like he expected his friend to be anywhere else. The bar wouldn't open for another hour, yet Marcus would be busy behind the grill and getting things ready.

Jace pushed the swinging door open, and yes, Marcus was in his element—chopping and dicing carrots.

"You're back!" Marcus said, smiling up at them.

"Hey, thanks for covering for us," he said, joining Marcus at his prep table.

"Ain't no biggie," Marcus responded easily. "It was good for you and Piper to get away for a few days."

Jace would have liked to have agreed but since they'd been kidnapped, tortured and more, he just nodded. "Still, I appreciate it. So no problems?"

"Nah, we did steady business. I had Brittany put the money in the safe. She started the order we'd need for next week and said she'd leave it on your desk."

"Good. Well, I'll let you get back to work," Jace told him, giving him a light slap on his shoulder.

The kitchen was gleaming and clean so he made his way back into the bar area.

Piper was behind the counter, getting the register ready. She looked like she belonged there. In all the time since he'd hired her, he hadn't realized it as much as he did gazing at her then.

She placed the bills inside before closing the drawer. When she twisted to sort through the bottles to her side, the short blue top she wore road up just a tad.

Jace knew how the skin on her back felt under his palms.

He hardened instantly thinking about how she would moan and say his name as he took her against the bar top.

Other than their very first time, they hadn't made love in the main bar. Even though he knew they couldn't at the moment with Marcus in the kitchen, that didn't keep him from wanting her.

Determined, he strolled across the old, scarred floor to her.

"Hey, Marcus doing okay?" she asked.

Instead of answering, Jace walked right up to her and kissed her strongly. She melted against him.

"Come on," he urged as he grabbed her hand.

"Where are we going?" she laughed. "Jace!"

"To my office," he told her, pulling harder.

The lights hadn't been turned on yet in the back but Jace knew the way well. He'd dreamed of having his own place for years before he'd been able to finally work it out.

"We have work to do," she stated, although she pushed the door open herself.

He flipped on the light. "We're the bosses. I don't think we'll get fired."

She was shaking her head at the same time as walking across the room to sit at his desk. "So you want me?" she teased.

"Yes."

Drawing her shirt over her head, she dropped it onto the black surface of the desk. "Well, come and get me."

He already had his hand on his zipper as he rushed to her.

Piper was working on her tennis shoes.

It was crazy. It was great.

She stood, grabbing at his shirt to help him tug it over his head. Jace slipped his arms around her back to unhook her bra.

"We have to hurry," Piper said breathlessly.

"Yeah," he agreed.

"So get naked," she ordered.

That was a demand he could follow.

It was a good thing none of the wait staff were scheduled to arrive yet. They shed their clothes fast before lunging toward one another. Piper nipped his bottom lip at the same time he grabbed her ass.

"I want you to ride me," he shared.

He dragged over his desk chair. Piper must have liked that idea. Her eyes shined when she pushed him into the leather. Jace held tightly while she straddled him.

"Come on," he encouraged.

Instead, Piper took her time grasping the base of his cock before lowering herself down. He had to bite his lip as her tight pussy clamped around his cock.

"Yes," he whispered, lifting his hips. "Yes."

She started to ride him. The sounds of flesh smacking flesh filled the room.

Jace kissed Piper as he started to come.

Chapter Eighteen

The house was quiet and even though she knew Mitch and Brian would be back soon, Piper couldn't help but worry. It had only been four days but she didn't like having either man so far away where she wasn't able to reach them quickly if they found trouble. Hearing the soft steps of her mate behind her, Piper didn't turn at the sound. Instead she snuggled back into his embrace when his arms bracketed her against the wooden porch rail.

"They'll be here soon," Jace told her. "Mitch called and said they were only about ten minutes away from town."

She nodded, Piper knew she was being stupid because they were both grown men, but she just couldn't get rid of the gut feeling that something was wrong. She'd woken with a dull ache of dread, and no matter how she tried to block the feeling, she just hadn't been able to.

"Cody should be here just as they're pulling up. I think Bobby will like that," Jace continued.

Piper agreed. Cody had stopped by the day that Bobby and Mitch had left for their trip and he and Jace had gotten to talking about how to add privacy to the back yard.

As Piper gazed out, she appreciated the additions that the two men had already made. There were more plants and trees to be added, causing Piper to be excited every time she thought about the end project.

Cody had shared the fact that Brian had asked him to transfer over to his unit. Since Cody knew about their wolf forms and proved loyal to the group, Brian was pushing to get him to sign on.

She was pretty sure that Cody would.

A car door slammed out the front. Taking a deep breath in, she recognized the scent. Cody had arrived and beaten Bobby and Mitch.

"Around back," she called out to him.

"He seems to be fitting in pretty well," Jace told her.

Chuckling, she turned in his arms. "I'd say. You two seem to almost be best buddies," she joked.

"Cody's a pretty cool guy once you get to know him. He still feels bad about getting us involved with Vince. I keep telling him there was no way he could have known what would happen. That's why he's so intent on helping with the yard. He wants to make it up to us."

Glancing to the side then once again enjoying the view Piper had to smile. "I'd say he's already made up for anything. Not that he has to."

Jace cupped her check, drawing her gaze back on him. "You have such a good heart. I wouldn't blame you if you did still feel uncomfortable around him."

"I don't," she assured Jace. "I would tell you if I did."

He skimmed his lips across hers but Piper wasn't going to settle for such a light touch. Grabbing a hold of his shoulders, she leaned up and pressed her mouth down harder.

He moaned, allowing her to slip her tongue inside.

Body responding, she shimmed even closer rubbing against the hard cock that was pushing into her stomach.

"Hey, guys! Oh!"

Piper ended the kiss with Jace slowly before peeking over his shoulder at Cody.

Cody had turned to the side and looked away.

"Hi, Cody," she greeted.

"Hey." He raised his hand. "I take it Bobby and Mitch aren't back yet?"

"Any minute," Jace supplied, releasing Piper.

"Good, I'm glad I beat them," Cody said. "I wanted to be waiting when Bobby arrived."

"Nope right on time. I was just admiring all the hard work that you've been doing. I can't thank you enough," Piper stated as she waved her hand around.

Cody shrugged. "It's no big deal. I enjoy the work, and you have such a beautiful yard that I get to play a little more."

As they spoke another car pulled up at the front of the house. She glanced over at Jace. "I think they're here."

"Let's go greet them."

Piper jumped down the three steps from the back porch to walk through the yard. Jace and Cody were behind her. She didn't wait for them. She swung the gate open and left it so they could get through.

She was just rounding the corner when Bobby opened the passenger door. Seeing his pale face and scenting the fear radiating from him, she growled fiercely before closing the distance at a run.

"What's wrong?" she asked, pulling him into her arms.

"We need to get inside," Mitch said from the other side of the vehicle.

Not having to be told twice, Piper wrapped her arm around Bobby's waist and propelled him forward. Once inside, she led Bobby to the couch in the living room. He was shaking against her.

Cody hovered in the doorway but when she waved him closer he quickly came.

"What is it?" she asked gently.

"I saw them," Bobby told her then buried his face in her neck.

She rubbed her hand down his back. He stopped shaking, and she knew that her calming effect was helping.

When Cody took a seat beside Bobby, he relaxed even further.

"Tell us," Jace demanded of Mitch.

"Just as we reached the city limits here, we saw a van pulled to the side of the road. I slowed down to see if I could offer them assistance when Bobby started to freak out. Said it was the guys that attacked his family and turned him."

Piper couldn't keep the gasp of surprise from slipping free. "Oh, honey." She hugged Bobby tighter.

"I know it was them. I could smell them."

"We believe you," Cody joined in reassuring Bobby.

"I had no doubt by the way he was acting that he was right. I slammed my foot down and tore out of there. I took several detours and drove in circles then headed here. I didn't want them to follow if they recognized Bobby."

"Good idea," Jace complimented.

"I knew I needed to bring Bobby here but I have to admit I really wanted to stop and confront them," Mitch confided.

"You can't!" Bobby practically yelled. "They'll kill you too!"

Piper tried to hush him but ended up letting Cody take Bobby as he sobbed. She stood and strolled over to Jace and Mitch. "Let's make Bobby some tea and discuss how to handle this," she suggested.

Cody nodded, pulling Bobby closer against him.

Now she knew why she'd felt so sick during the day. Had she had some sort of premonition about Bobby's attackers?

Jace was filling the tea kettle with water as Mitch hunched over the island when she entered the kitchen. Spotting Mitch's fists curled tightly, she went to him first and hugged him.

Mitch's shoulders fell. "Thanks."

"No problem," she replied sincerely. She liked being able to help.

"I just wanted to go back there so damn bad. Bobby is terrified and he shouldn't have to live like that."

"Do you think they followed him here?" Piper asked quietly. She didn't want Bobby to overhear them although he probably still could.

"Why else would they be in Blue Cove?" Jace questioned. "Joe followed you and I'd bet anything that those two are tracking Bobby."

"What are we going to do?" she wondered out loud. There was no way they would get close to Bobby. Between her, Jace, Cody and Mitch they would protect him. But Bobby shouldn't be trapped in the house either.

Jace had printed out information on San Diego University in the hope that Bobby would go back to school. They wanted him to be able to enjoy his life. This new threat would derail that plan.

"We take care of them," Mitch stated forcefully.

"I have to agree with Mitch. We need to find them before they figure out where Bobby is. If they can track him hundreds of miles, as small as this town it won't be too long before they show up here."

"What about calling Brian?" Mitch suggested. "He has more experience with werewolves, so he might have some ideas."

"That's a good idea." Piper jumped at the thought. Instead of going into a fight unprepared, they could call on her new Pack member.

The tea kettle started to whistle.

"Let's take this to Bobby, and while Piper is calling Brian, why don't Mitch and I go back to where they spotted the van?" Jace said.

Piper jerked back. "By yourselves?"

"We won't confront them. I just want to see if they're still there. If not, maybe we can get the location of where they're staying."

"But you won't do anything yet?" she pressed.

Smiling, Jace set the mug he'd been filling down on the counter. "No, I promise. We'll wait to hear what Brian has to say. After that, we'll all sit together with Bobby and make a plan."

Piper crossed the room quickly, and grabbed Jace's chin. "Be careful—both of you."

"We will," he reassured her.

"Go out the back. I'll take Bobby his drink before calling Brian."

"We'll be back before you know it."

Piper sure the hell hoped so. She squatted down behind the island, burying her face in her hands. She wanted to scream and punch someone but knew she had to remain calm. The others needed her to soothe them.

Breathe in, breathe out. Maybe she needed to take up yoga or something. Closing her eyes, she tried again. *Breathe in, breathe out*. Over and over she repeated the act until she felt centered.

Piper pushed herself off the ground and stood. She squealed, spotting Cody and Bobby in the doorway.

"Shit! You scared me!"

Bobby offered her a shy smile. His eyes were still red but he looked like he was holding it together better. "I wanted to see if I could help with the beverages."

"Sit." She waved him over. "I got it."

When they both settled at the island, she set the cups in front of them. Next she pushed the sugar where they could reach it before turning to the fridge for lemons and milk.

Once she had everything, she poured herself a mug. Although she'd never drunk tea until she'd moved in with Jace, she was beginning to really enjoy having a cup every once in a while.

Jace had picked up the habit when he'd been overseas and still appreciated the drink. He even ordered his tea from a fabulous company in the UK that had some of the best.

"You're going to call Brian?" Bobby asked while he blew on his drink.

"I think he'll be able to advise us on the best way to handle this."

"That's smart," Cody spoke up.

Bobby glanced from her to Cody. "I just hate getting more people involved in my mess."

"Hey." She reached over and placed her hand over his. "This is not your fault. Those guys attacked you. We just want to make sure they can't hurt you again."

"I know. I wish I could do it myself, though."

Piper understood. Would she have had the closure she possessed if Jace had killed Joe instead of her? She didn't think so.

Protecting her mate against her own demon that had tormented her still haunted her but she also knew she could protect them both.

"We won't do anything without you," Piper told him. "You'll be involved in every way, so if there is something you want to do, just let me know."

Nodding, he smiled a little before taking a sip of his tea.

* * * *

Jace opened the door to Brian and Katy. "Come on in. Thanks for coming so fast."

"Of course. If one member in the Pack has a problem, we all do," Brian told him.

Letting them pass him in the hall, Jace made sure to lock the door back up tightly. "We're in the kitchen."

"This is a nice house," Katy commented, as she traveled through the living room. "I love the flowers in the front."

"Wait till you see the back," Jace told her.

When they reached the kitchen, Piper was already pulling down new mugs. They had switched from tea to coffee over the last half hour as they waited for Brian to arrive.

"Hey, Bobby." Brian patted Bobby's back as he passed. "How're you holding up?"

"Okay, I guess."

Brian nodded before turning to Jace. "Piper said you were trying to find the van?"

"Yeah, they'd already left the spot that Mitch saw them at. We drove around for a while but couldn't pick up their trail."

"What's the van look like?" Katy questioned.

"It's an older model black Chevy van. The windows were really dark."

Jace didn't miss the look that was exchanged between Brian and Katy. "What?"

"We saw a van like that up the street."

Bobby stiffened as Piper dropped the bag of sugar she'd been refilling the canister with.

"That was fast. How did they already track him down?" Cody asked.

"They're on the block?" Bobby enquired at the same time.

"It's okay," Mitch told them. "I say we go take them down."

"We can't!" Bobby exclaimed.

"It's okay, Bobby. You can stay here," Jace told them.

"But…" Bobby started.

Jace nodded for Mitch to move ahead.

"Wait!" Piper called out, stopping Jace. "Bobby, what would you like to do?"

"We can't just attack them. We don't really know what they came for," Bobby said.

"But they turned you," Katy argued.

"I know. But I think we should let them come to us. If we go and just kill them, that makes us just as bad as they are."

Jace had to give Bobby credit. The kid had a point. As much as he wanted to go straight out there and rip them apart, they weren't animals, even if they could shift into wolves. "What do you suggest?"

"What if I went out back? If they think I'm alone, maybe they'll come after me?"

"You're not going alone," Piper demanded.

"Piper has a point. They'd never believe that you'd be out there by yourself," Mitch agreed.

"And they aren't getting that close to Bobby," Piper declared.

Jace could see Piper's protective instinct flaring. Their connection allowed him to feel how upset she was. "What if Bobby and Piper went out back and saw if they could lure the two guys here."

"We can wait in here and see what happens. They could always shift to get away," Brian suggested.

Jace glanced from Bobby to Piper to see them both nodding.

"Sounds like a plan," Cody agreed.

"Might as well do this," Bobby stated, as he pushed himself up from his stool.

Jace walked around the island to wrap his arm around Piper's waist. "We'll be right inside. Maybe you can act like you're showing Bobby the additions of plants and just keep an ear out."

She rose onto her toes to gently kiss him. "I will."

Jace deepened the kiss, not caring that they weren't alone. If Piper was going to put herself in harm's way, he was going to get a decent lip lock.

She felt good in his arms and even better gripping the muscles of his arms. Their tongues twined and slid against one another until someone cleared their throat.

"Be careful."

"I promise."

Watching Piper and Bobby walk out through the sliding glass door was harder than Jace would have imagined. He knew that they were only outside—steps away from where he waited—but he couldn't help the feeling of nausea that made his gut clench.

Brian walked to the long blinds, closing them.

"What are you doing?" he snapped at his friend.

"I figured if they peeked over at Piper and Bobby and saw us in the kitchen, they might not make their move."

"We can't see them either, though," Cody complained.

Glad he wasn't alone in his worry, he appreciated Cody being there with him.

"It might help if we opened the window above the sink," Katy suggested. "We could at least hear if something happens."

Jace sprinted over and yanked the panel up.

Piper had her arm through Bobby's as they walked from one tree to the next under the guise of checking out the plants.

"Anything?" Bobby whispered.

"No, try to relax. We have five people inside who are going to make sure we're not hurt. Plus, you are quick as lightening if you have to transform, so that will help."

"I just wish this was over with. Maybe I should have let them go after the guys?"

She turned him so he had to face her. "You did the right thing. There is no telling what would have happened if we attacked their van. We don't know what kind of weapons they have and someone could have gotten hurt."

"Yeah."

"Plus with the privacy back here, there is less of a chance of the neighbors seeing what is going on," she added.

"I know I should want them dead, but I want them to pay. Death seems too easy for them."

"That's my guy." Piper hugged him. "Brian is prepared to take them back to the base and make them answer for what they did. He already spoke with his captain and they even have a cell for them. We can't call the regular police, so this is the best option."

"Okay." Bobby squeezed her again before he released her. "It really is gorgeous back here. Cody is talented."

"I love it. And Jace is having so much fun with him."

"I can't believe how much they did in such a short amount of time," Bobby told her.

Shrugging, Piper drew Bobby to the chairs they'd set under one of the oak trees. "Once they started, I couldn't get them to stop. The more they talk about their plans, the better picture I get on what they're trying to accomplish."

Piper sat where she had a good look at the gate entrance. Bobby took the seat beside her and she could see how much he wanted to look around them.

"It's okay."

"Why haven't they come out here?" he enquired.

"They're probably watching, making sure no one is coming to join us. Why don't you tell me more about your trip? I wouldn't mind hearing more about the zoo in Arizona."

As Bobby started to tell her how the other animals had reacted to him and Mitch, the air around them began to cool. Piper wished she'd grabbed a light jacket before coming out.

Just as Bobby was seemingly starting to forget why they were out there and was really going into his story, Piper heard a crunch from the gate area.

Bobby hadn't seemed to notice so she didn't alert him. Instead she glanced back at the house quickly.

They had closed the blinds but she noticed the kitchen window had been opened. That was smart thinking.

Peering back at Bobby, she tried to pay attention to his visit to the Grand Canyon. He was so excited that she almost lost herself in the story.

"Well, well, well what have we here?"

Piper startled for show. "Who are you? What are you doing back here?" she questioned the man who had swung the gate open.

"Piper!" Bobby called her name as he grabbed her arm.

"Ah look, Craig. Our little friend remembers us."

Craig grinned. "I bet he does, Nicky. Hey, buddy, did you miss us?"

Fury rolled over Piper and it took everything in her not to jump at them. How dare they come into her property and taunt Bobby.

"Listen here. I don't know who you are, but you'd better leave," she said between clenched teeth."

"Feisty," Craig said laughing. "I like that."

Well, Piper had warned them.

The two strangers had been steadily advancing.

"Come here, boy," Nicky demanded, leering at Bobby.

"No," Bobby stated firmly. "And you're trespassing. If you don't leave now, I'm calling the cops."

Pride swamped Piper as Bobby stood up to them.

"Lookie who grew some balls," Craig goaded.

Movement behind the men drew Piper's attention as Mitch and Brian came in the yard from the front. She grinned at the strangers. "We did warn you."

Before they could figure out what she meant, the patio door opened and Jace raced out with Katy on his heels. Katy had shifted into her wolf form and was growling furiously.

Craig and Nicky stepped back and right into the path of Brian and Mitch.

It didn't take long for Craig and Nicky to be on the ground secured with handcuffs that Brian had brought with him. There was a lot of cursing and fists flying, but they were no match for highly trained soldiers.

"Anything you want to say to them?" Piper asked Bobby.

He nodded while slowly striding forward. He crouched down so they had to look at him. "You're going to pay—for what you did to my parents and for what you did to me. And I'm going to enjoy every minute of it."

Chapter Nineteen

The large black wolf darted in front of Piper and she had just enough time to change direction to avoid a collision. Mitch was getting more comfortable around the others as they continued to have weekly runs at the base.

Piper growled in warning at him but could tell that Mitch didn't even realize where he'd been heading. He remained chasing Katy across the expansive field.

Shaking her head, she loped back around to find her mate.

"That was a close one," Jace said, burying his hand in the thick fur of her neck.

She panted in agreement.

Jace started to rub her down, and she didn't really care what the rest of the Pack was doing. She just wanted Jace's hands on her. The night had darkened the area and only the addition of light they'd have installed around the shifting area aided Jace in being able to see them at all.

"One of the wolves took out a couple of the new shrubs we planted," Cody observed from his spot next to Jace.

Since she was pretty sure Bobby was involved in the tussle, she knew Cody wouldn't be too upset. It had been Bobby's idea to fix up their running area and he'd helped Cody and Jace plant and set trees, bushes and even flowers.

Their little piece of the base had really started to grow and blossom.

"I think we'll need to set up rules for the Pack so we don't have to keep replacing stuff," Jace said.

Piper licked his hand in apology.

"It's fine, babe. As long as you're enjoying herself."

She loved coming out here. Sure this was only the fifth time but as the weeks passed, she felt more and more comfortable. Becoming the Alpha of the small group gave her a purpose in life.

Mitch's transfer into Brian's unit had helped keep him around more, although he was finally seriously thinking about retiring and buying into Anderson's Loft. Mitch and Marcus wanted to expand from the bar and make it a restaurant that would also be open during lunch.

Bobby would be starting school soon and while he remained living with her and Jace, Piper would bet that before the semester started, he'd be moved in with Cody. She'd miss seeing him every day but with the military members of the Pack spending more time at the house, Piper didn't think she'd have time to be too depressed about it.

Ready to call it a night, she gave Jace's hand a nudge then rolled back onto her paws. She took a few short steps and lifted her muzzle, letting out a long howl.

The answering call came quickly.

She stood guard, still in animal form as the others shifted. It wasn't until the last member of her Pack was human again that she began her own transformation.

Jace strolled over handing her a pair of lounge pants and a T-shirt so she dressed quickly.

"Thank you, everyone, for coming out. We'll see you for breakfast in the morning," she announced.

Spinning to Jace, she grabbed a hold of his hand to pull him toward the barracks. As they'd done after the first run with the Pack, all of them would stay the night. They'd have a quick breakfast with the Pack as well as the human members of Brian's team before they returned home. The humans weren't considered Pack but they had become friends.

"Did you have fun?" Jace asked, as she led him away from the yard.

"Yes, each time I shift, it has gotten easier."

Nodding, he released her hand to throw his arm around her neck. "You're faster also."

"I know." She couldn't keep the excitement hidden. And why should she? It had been a long time coming, but she was finally at ease being able to turn into a wolf.

They reached the entrance of the building, close to their room, so Piper dropped her hand down to Jace's waist.

He skimmed his lips across her ear, causing her to shiver.

She peeked behind her and saw the others were still in the field. Taking a chance to be a little naughty, she slipped her hand into the back waistband of Jace's pants.

"Feeling adventurous?" Jace teased.

"Get me to the room and I'll show you how much," she replied.

About the Author

Crissy Smith lives in Texas with her husband, daughter, and three Labrador retrievers. The three dogs love to curl up under her computer desk and nap while she writes. It doesn't leave a lot of room for her but what's a woman to do?

When not writing or reading, she enjoys hunting, camping and shooting. But she has a girly side too and is addicted to pedicures and coffee.

She has been writing since she was a teenager and still loves everything to do with the paranormal. Her stories and characters all have a place in her heart. She loves the Alpha male, the dominant werewolf, and the Master vampire, which find their way in most of her books.

Learn more about the characters she has created at her website where they have their very own page. It will be updated from time to time to let you know what's going on with them. Also you can find out who will be in the next book.

Crissy loves to hear from readers. You can find her contact information, website and author biography at http://www.totallybound.com.

Totally Bound Publishing

Home of Erotic Romance